This story is a work of fictio[n]
and any similarities to actual [...]

ISBN: 978-1-998763-25-2

WHAT HIDES IN THE CUPBOARDS

CASSONDRA WINDWALKER

CHAPTER ONE

"Son of a cinnamon stick," Hesper yowled, scrambling out of the way as the heavy box slipped from her stiff fingers. She heard Richard muffling a snort of laughter, but when she glanced out the open door, he was nowhere to be seen. "Wise man," she said.

Her ridiculous vanilla swears were all his fault, anyway. In the early days of their marriage, barely out of high school, they'd both sported the blue tongues of seasoned sailors. Late nights poring over college textbooks and long hours at their full-time jobs hadn't softened their approach to life, even when Hesper dropped out of school three-quarters of the way through her Fine Arts degree. But once Richard secured his first job as an elementary school music teacher, he decided he'd better adjust his vocabulary for fear of an inopportune slip.

His alternative curses had been so preposterous, they'd somehow been contagious. Soon enough Hesper had gone from laughing at him to echoing him. How many nights had they spent drinking cheap beer and cackling like hyenas as they proposed and rejected one ridiculous substitution after another? Now the silly euphemisms slipped free without a second thought.

My husband has ruined me, Hesper mused without regret.

Luckily this particular box was all books and nothing breakable. Not that there was much hope of pulling off this move without breaking at least a few things. She was all done with her physical therapy—at least, she'd told her therapist in no uncertain terms she was done and then moved 1,200 miles away. Four months was long enough, as far as she was concerned. Muscle spasms like the one that had just pirouetted the box out of her hands and some stiffness in her fingers persisted, but she was determined to work out the rest on her own.

If she was honest with herself, and she generally was, Hesper was terrified that her fingers would continue their stubbornly wooden responses. Going back week after week to see the sympathy on her therapist's face and listen to platitudes in tones intended to calm and soothe was more than she could handle. At this point, it was all up to her body—either it would respond to the exercises and treatment, or it wouldn't.

As a potter, losing the function of her hands, even in small measure, was the stuff of nightmares. How many attempts had she smashed back into lumps of accusing almostness, all her inspiration evaporating into tears and rage? Richard reassured her that she was simply impatient—the accident had been only weeks ago, really. And she'd already regained so much movement. When she'd told him she wasn't going back to therapy, he'd rolled his eyes and shook his head.

"You'll be fine," he told her. "Probably working with the clay is the best therapy, anyway. Give yourself time."

Time. Time had become a monster she never realized lurked with such malevolence in the shadow of every hour. Even the word tasted sour on her tongue.

That was part of why she'd come here, wasn't it? To fall out of time entirely? The cycles of the desert had nothing to do with clocks and calendars. Here she could rise and fall with the sunrises and sunsets, unbothered by the ceaseless rumbling of wheels on the road, horns and sirens and voices. And teachers were in such high demand, Richard could work anywhere. Although this little hacienda was islanded in what felt like perfect stillness, they were only twenty minutes from Santa Fe.

Hesper retrieved the box and set it on the massive, solid-wood dining table the previous owner had left behind. She retwisted her long hair into the clip it kept escaping. She glanced longingly at the cooler full of sodas and beers that held the front door propped open. She'd made a deal with herself—every ten boxes or pieces of furniture, she could take a drink. Luckily she hadn't brought that much. She tended to be ruthless when it came to closing chapters in her life.

She'd never suffered a moment's regret when she dropped out of college, regardless of how friends and family

9

had protested. She possessed none of Richard's inclination to teach, and it wasn't as if art collectives or museums hired fine art graduates to sit in a studio and create for them. The idea of working as a docent or curator made her soul shrivel. That would be the equivalent of a sommelier reduced to stocking hotel mini-bars, as far as she was concerned. If she were really lucky, she might get a residency somewhere for a few months, but if her portfolio were strong enough, she could work with galleries on her own. Between school and work, she hardly had time to spend with the clay these days at all.

She'd sold all her books back and used the money to pay bills. She worked like a beast the next year and a half while Richard finished his requirements. When he got his first teaching job, she quit working and focused entirely on her art.

Objects of significance, books, the tools of her trade— these were all she really cared about. She'd never been much of a homemaker, as Richard could attest. If it had color or told a story, she found it a place, but things like furniture, clothes, curtains, the kind of cars they drove, didn't matter to her. A happy synchronicity with poverty, as it turned out. When she'd packed for this move, she'd sold or donated or thrown away at least half of what she owned.

A handful of sweaters were all that remained of the masses of warm-weather clothes the fierce winters of northern Illinois had required. Their bed, of course, had made the trip, a dresser, some bookshelves. Her wheel and kiln. A couple boxes of dishes and pans sufficed just fine. Richard's wardrobe had received the same culling treatment as her own. Her favorites, like the college hoodie he used to wear while running and the threadbare Ramones t-shirt that still smelled of his skin, were necessities. His desk, too, had made the trip.

Thanks to her ruthlessness, she'd managed to pack everything into a single moving truck, her little car on a trailer hitched behind.

By the time she got everything stacked inside her new home, she was sweaty and sticky and sore, but triumphant. She'd managed to unload it all before the trucking company closed in town. She drove back to Santa Fe, dropped off the truck and trailer, and drove her Subie back. She stopped for a hot pizza and a box of breadsticks on her way home.

Home. That sounded right. Good, even. The apartment in Evanston hadn't felt like home for what seemed like forever now. But this place—this place sang to her.

She and Richard had taken their honeymoon in Taos. Not really, of course—kids barely out of high school didn't get honeymoons. But that's what they'd named the vacation they'd given themselves Richard's first summer after a year of teaching. Hesper had always been fascinated by the artists of the Southwest, and the desert held a strange seductive appeal for a child of the wintry northern plains.

Nothing about New Mexico had disappointed. From the rugged mountains to the spectacular sunsets to the singing silence of the desert arroyos, she'd been entranced from the moment they arrived. Walking through the galleries and markets, talking to every artist who would spare her the time, she had the sense of standing on the brink of more mystery than any one lifetime could ever perceive, much less unravel.

Richard had leapt into the experience with both feet, right beside her, his hand holding fast to hers. Every moment had been a sensual feast—eating the food, walking the trails, breathing the sage-and-juniper air, making love several times a day, wherever they found themselves. He'd been as fascinated as she was. They would walk back to their hotel under starry skies, their tongues loose with tequila and strange tales, their ears full of live music, sandaled feet dusty with the adventures of the day. The land itself existed in a void of time and distance, closer to far-flung galaxies than to any place on earth, and redolent with songs last sung by strangers dead a thousand years. It seemed impossible they'd ever lived anywhere else, would ever leave.

But honeymoons don't last forever, and once they'd returned to Evanston, Taos faded into only a place he'd once been, as far as Richard was concerned. Hesper hadn't been able to forget the allure of the desert, though.

And now, seven years later, here they were.

It took nearly every ounce of self-control in her body, but Hesper resisted the deliciously gooey hot-cheese fragrance wafting from the greasy box until she got home to Richard. No electricity yet, so they set up a powerful flashlight like a candle on the dining table. Instead of chairs, the table sported wide slab benches, painted in peeling shades of turquoise, orange, yellow, and blue. Hesper sank onto one of them with a grateful sigh, popping the top off a bottle of sour cherry beer and grabbing a slice of pizza.

Richard's eyes were warm as he gazed at her through the garish flashlight glow. "Welcome home, honey," he said. His low voice licked along her skin like a dancing matchlight flame. "It's been a long road."

"But we made it," she said around a mouthful of doughy crust and mozzarella. He laughed.

Something in his laugh jangled, and the room tilted. The pizza that had been so savory turned to cardboard in her mouth, and Hesper coughed, choking. She shook her head, willing the walls to hold still, the light to stop its crazy flickering.

"I'm tired," she said abruptly, pushing herself up from the table and leaving the pizza and beer behind.

Richard said nothing, his eyes shadowed as they followed her exit.

She stumbled into the dark space that would be their

bedroom, stripping haphazardly as she went. "Mastodon-muncher," she swore under her breath at the sluggish fingers tripping over her zipper.

Thank goodness she'd piled up all the loose blankets on the mattress and box spring pushed into the corner of the room. She could set up the bedframe and headboard tomorrow. Now all she wanted was sleep. Sleep and sweet, blessed forgetfulness.

Dreams had nearly claimed her when she heard Richard's soft footfalls in the hall. He navigated the obstacle course of boxes and random piles in the pitch darkness without a misstep. His clothes whispered away from his form, and Hesper sighed with relief when he lowered himself beside her, wrapping her naked body tightly in his own. His hands, though, were cold, so cold, on her breasts as she slipped into a deep sleep.

CHAPTER TWO

Hesper woke huddled in a heap of blankets. Richard had always been an earlier riser than she was. She liked to say she kept artist's hours. Which meant she kept no hours at all.

Cold pizza and lukewarm beer waited for her where she'd left them on the table. She shrugged. Breakfast for dinner, dinner for breakfast, what was the difference? Menu assignments were arbitrary distinctions of culture. She downed a bottle and scarfed two slices of pizza before wandering through the house, formulating a plan of attack.

The electrician she'd spoken to over the phone would be here sometime later this morning. She checked her phone. It still had a little battery life left. If she got desperate, she could always start up the car and charge it there. She should have gotten one of those little battery charging packs, but she hadn't been that organized when she left Evanston.

That reminded her. She'd better check to be sure that the solar panels she'd had delivered had actually arrived. The realtor had agreed to come out and lock them up in the shed for her.

Hesper located the keys under a box on the kitchen counter. She slipped into a pair of sandals and padded outside to the little hovel that passed for a shed. Sure enough, the panels were neatly stacked against a cobwebby wall. She left the door standing open and dropped the keys into the top pocket of the denim overalls she wore over a threadbare tank top. She and Richard had long held fantasies of becoming off-grid hippies, but sustainable living in the big city was more mythical than unicorns, despite what the farmers' market and hemp collectives tried to claim.

Deep breath in. Deep breath out. *Be where you are,* she reminded herself.

The air tasted so sweet and fresh. It was like breathing in raw animus. Nothing like the wet, muggy, pollution-drenched air she was used to. The sun hung just over the horizon, already warming the day. Hesper took a moment to drink in the sight of her new home. She'd been in such a hurry when she'd pulled in yesterday, she'd hardly looked around.

The realtor had thought the place something of an albatross, but Hesper absolutely loved it. Luckily, she had cellphone reception out here, but there was no electricity. Water was supplied by a well. The house itself looked part of the desert, with thick stucco walls, rugged timbers, and a roof of red clay tile. A copse of stunted trees wrapped the house in blessed shade.

A crumbling wall encircled a broad flagstone courtyard, and Hesper intended to set up her foot-powered wheel and her kiln there. Her electric wheel she would keep inside. Eventually, she wanted to experiment with the micaceous clays that could be found in the Manzano Mountains, about

16

an hour or so away. She planned to build a wood-fired kiln so she could incorporate the qualities of the smoke and ash into glittering mica. How magical would that be? People sometimes imagined the ceramic arts were a poor cousin to the others—mechanical and crude and laborious. But Hesper knew it was pure alchemy. As some mythologies claimed on behalf of the gods, the potter breathed life into clay, transformed the very dirt into a sort of eternity.

But that undertaking would have to wait. Hesper had much to do, and much to learn, in the meantime.

A smile crept irrepressibly across her face. She could do this. She could be happy here.

The realtor had had her doubts. It's very isolated, she'd warned Hesper. No neighbors. No corner bar or cozy restaurants.

I'm coming for the desert, Hesper had explained. Surely that wasn't so uncommon. Artists of every ilk had made mecca of this desert for decades.

I suppose that makes sense, the realtor had conceded. The previous owner was an artist, too. A painter. He came from the big city as well. He didn't last long, though.

Moved back to the city? Hesper had wondered. Looking at the house now, that seemed impossible to imagine. Who would leave this place, so steeped in the sacred, for the relentless yammering of the city?

No, the realtor had told her grimly. In fact, I'm required

by law to divulge certain facts about the property before you make an offer. The previous owner died here, in the house. By his own hand.

Oh.

Well, that was unfortunate, Hesper thought. No doubt that accounted for the low price, that and the lack of utilities and general remoteness. Unfortunate for him, but fortunate for me.

Every inch of the earth is a grave, Hesper had told the realtor matter-of-factly, and promptly made an offer ten thousand dollars below the asking price. She was well aware the place had already been on the market for over a year.

And now it was hers. Hers and Richard's. A safe, still, oasis of silence where they could live and love, and she could create. Warm fingers of sunlight settled on her shoulders, peace sinking into her bones.

Enough wool-gathering. It was time to get the house in order. And maybe have another piece of pizza.

She tackled the furniture first, placing the bookshelves and dressers and assembling the bed. She'd gotten rid of the couch back in Evanston, but she dragged her cozy old recliner into the living room, situating it in front of the wide picture window and tossing a nubbly green-and-gold blanket over it. She unfolded a card table and shook out the pieces of a new wooden jigsaw puzzle. Manipulating those intricate little shapes was no mean feat for her stiff fingers, so it was good exercise. And with no internet service out here yet, she'd need something to occupy her during the long evening hours before sleep. Something to pretend at companionship.

The phone rang while she was sorting through the kitchen boxes.

"Hi, Ginny," Hesper answered as she continued to pull glasses, plates, and pans from the boxes.

"Hi, Hesper," Richard's sister said with cheer that had been forced so long, Hesper hardly even noticed it anymore. "How's the new house? Tell me all about it."

Hesper had bought the place long-distance, sight unseen, aside from the photos on the internet, much to her sister-in-law's dismay.

"It's fantastic. Absolutely everything I hoped for. Just two bedrooms, but the rooms are all huge. And you would love this kitchen. Big, dark wood cabinets, painted tiles, rounded doorways. Exposed timbers. Zuni effects. A courtyard perfect for my work."

"But no electricity?"

"I have an electrician coming today to install solar panels and get the battery system set up for me, whatever that looks like. The place was already wired for solar power, but I guess the original panels got stolen. It was sitting empty for quite a while, you know."

"Yeah, you told me what happened there. I'm worried about you, Hesper. That seems really grim, especially after everything you've been through. Doesn't the place just feel sad? I don't like to think of you lonely out there."

Unlike her wife Felka, whose primary concern had been ghosts, Ginny didn't have a superstitious bone in her body. But that didn't mean she hadn't had serious—and loudly voiced—reservations about this move.

Hesper laughed lightly, pushing her hair back. "If every place that somebody ever died in felt sad, we'd all be drowning in despair. And of course I won't be lonely. I have Richard."

Silence stretched between them.

Finally, Ginny cleared her throat. "Well, I wanted to give you a heads-up. Felka and I sent you a little housewarming gift. It should be delivered tomorrow. You might think it's a little weird when it gets there, but give me a call and I'll explain everything."

Naturally Ginny's gift would come with a story, Hesper thought, grinning. Ginny was a librarian, and she was constitutionally incapable of a shallow gift.

"All right, I will. But I better get off the phone. I don't have that much battery left, and the electrician might call if he gets lost or something."

"Sounds good. I love you, girl. Take good care of yourself." Ginny clicked off.

Hesper set the phone down on the kitchen table, where—hopefully!—she wouldn't lose it. Just since arriving yesterday, she'd misplaced the thing at least six times. She tended to be absent-minded under the best of circumstances, and adjusting to an entirely new environment apparently added a whole new squirrel level to her general scatterbrain.

Hesper was grateful Ginny's voice had broken into her day. For a moment, it had been as if the other woman were actually in the room with her, sharing the excitement of this new adventure. Hesper didn't know what would have become of her these few months since the accident without her sister-in-law. They'd always been fond of each other. Hesper knew she herself could be a difficult person, often drifting into a distant, remote state where Richard didn't understand her and couldn't reach her, but Ginny was the opposite—warm, wise, watchful. She saw what others were blind to. What had been an easy affection between the two women had become a lifeline to Hesper in these dark days. Ginny called, usually every other day at least, and her voice centered Hesper, brought her back to herself.

Back to hope, whose location on Hesper's map kept getting erased.

Hesper shook her head at the thought. *A gift.* A little bubble of excitement floated up through her veins. There was no telling with Ginny what that might mean. But it was sure to be a small patch of joy.

What had she been doing again? Oh, yes. Time to sort

the kitchen. Hesper was a one-and-done kind of woman when it came to organization, so wherever stuff landed was where it stayed, whether that made sense to household gods or visiting guests or Richard or anyone else. Life was short, perilously short, Hesper knew. Why waste time and spirit fussing about the most efficient placement of a wine glass or a towel when there were the stars to wonder about and now, in her new home, lizards to consult?

Such a pale green denizen sat on the edge of the sink now, its head cocked as it gazed her with a tiny bright eye.

"Oh, hello," Hesper murmured. "Have you come to help me? Perhaps you're here to bless my kitchen?"

Barely longer than her middle finger, the creature emitted the funniest little squeak and then raced down the cabinet, across the kitchen floor, and disappeared. He moved so quickly, it was like watching water. She laughed, delighted. She wasn't sure why the notion of lizards in her house was a pleasant one when she'd been absolutely ruthless about the possibility of any rodents in the apartment in Evanston, but whatever.

"It's different," she said firmly to the air. "Entirely different."

Now that she had infestations on her mind, though, she flung open all the kitchen cabinets at once and peered anxiously inside. No signs of mice or scorpions, but plenty of cobwebs. She filled the sink with soapy water and retrieved a rag for scrubbing before she set her clean dishes in there.

"I think whoever lived here before was a little confused about the purposes of shelf paper," she murmured.

Instead of placing the paper on the floors of the cabinets, someone had pasted the shelf paper up over the interior doors. One of the things Hesper had loved most about the house when the realtor had emailed her the photos had been the beautiful dark wood cabinets with their twisting, gleaming grain. They reminded Hesper of the juniper trees outside. Who would cover up that gorgeous wood with hideous pastel-flowered shelf paper that looked like it came from some grandma's underwear drawer?

She didn't want to get sucked into home improvement. She wanted to unpack and settle into her new home as quickly as possible, so she could allow herself to disappear into the desert the way Georgia O'Keefe had and just become her art and nothing else.

Maybe Georgia would've taken issue with that description of her life, but that was what Hesper wanted, at any rate. She wanted to be throwing clay, not scraping wallpaper and setting up chaises first at this angle, then at that.

But the shelf paper was so very garish. An affront to the natural beauty of the rest of the house, which rose as a part of the desert rather than a rebellion against it. Leaving it felt like leaving a hand clamped over the mouth of the house.

Hesper sighed. Hopefully this wouldn't take too long.

She was in luck. Whoever had put it up, had been in a hurry and hadn't done more than glue the corners. The hideous stuff peeled away like wrapping paper.

"Ham sandwiches!" Hesper exclaimed, nearly falling backward off the stepladder.

A painted face stared at her from the cabinet door, its dark eyes as vivid as the eyes in a mirror.

Catching her breath, Hesper scrabbled at the edges of the paper to reveal the painting in its entirety. It wasn't a portrait, exactly, it turned out. The artist's style was something between cubism and impressionism, if there was such a thing. Images she could almost but not quite identify floated in the background. Only the face of a little boy was clear, almost drifting free of the rest of the painting. His eyes were at once sad and accusatory, and what should have been endearing was instead somehow frightening.

The realtor said the man who killed himself here was an artist. Could he have been the one who did this?

Had to have been, didn't he?

Hesper retreated to a seat on the dining table bench after grabbing a beer from the cooler. She drank thirstily, her eyes fixed on the gaze of the boy in her cabinet. No wonder somebody had papered over that. The realtor, she was sure. To say it was startling was an understatement.

Unwillingly her eyes drifted to the other cabinet doors.

Standing open, their shelf-paper gags demanding to be torn down. A queer dread seized her belly. Her imagination, never a slacker, conjured clawing hands tearing their way free of the crawling pink roses, heads tossing and eyes rolling from their paper prisons.

The desert was nothing if not the land of ghosts and demons, wraiths and skinwalkers. No way was she going to invite the ire of any bad juju by leaving spirits in chains, however fanciful that might be. She sprang back up, downing the last of her beer, and tore away the paper from every other cabinet door.

"Ham sandwiches," she whispered again, shaken to her core.

The same child stared at her from a total of ten doors. His perspective varied, so that he gazed up from the lower cabinets and down from the upper ones. Wherever she stood in the kitchen, his attention, prismed through the myriad images, remained fastened on her.

No two were quite the same. The backgrounds, the colors, varied. As did his expression. Here he was frightened, here he was forlorn. Here he laughed, but Hesper thought she caught something cruel in his smile, a twist doubly menacing against the foil of his innocence and youth. Five years old? Maybe six or seven? Hesper didn't have much experience with children.

Richard wanted children, would have been happy to start

five years ago even. Hesper didn't begrudge him that at all. He was so good with children, with people of all ages, really. He took everyone as they were and found something to celebrate in that. She loved to watch him with the little ones on Open School nights or at the hilariously inept elementary music performances staged for doting parents. Hesper couldn't help pitying women who didn't know how sexy kindness could be. Let others moon after superheroes and secret spies. Give her an elementary school teacher or a soup kitchen volunteer any day.

Of course, she hadn't been the only woman drawn to Richard and his tender hands, had she?

Ruthlessly she shoved the thought aside. She'd promised herself she wouldn't think about that anymore. She'd promised Richard.

Seized by a sudden idea, she left the kitchen as it was. What about the bathroom cabinets? The closet doors?

Paper. Paper pasted everywhere. And behind it all, that same boy. Only not the same. In every representation, he was as singular and unique as any person caught in an instant of time. What remained identical to each was the startling vivacity of his eyes, the way they caught and held her own, whether they wept or winced or sparkled.

Licorice sticks, but the house was hot. The thick stucco walls provided some relief, and still, not a breath of wind whispered through the open windows and doors today. That electrician couldn't get here soon enough. A fan would make a world of difference. The thought of that water cooler outside her bedroom rattling to life was downright orgasmic.

The house that had been a haven had become something else with the revelation of the boy. It was as if the house wanted something from her. Demanded something. A chill swept her sweat-soaked skin.

"Richard?" she said, gently pushing open the door to the second bedroom where she'd set up his desk. Just the sight of him there, bent over his books and papers, eased her soul.

He spun to face her, his too-long dark hair falling over his glasses like it always did. Deep blue eyes that were never cold met her own.

"What is it, baby?"

"I don't know," she said, crossing the room to sit at his feet and rest her head on his knee. "What if this was a terrible mistake? What if we shouldn't have come here?"

He stroked her hair, and she felt all her being existed only where his fingers touched her skin. "Why would you say that? You know how happy we were when we came to Taos. And you've dreamed of the desert ever since."

"There's all these weird paintings closed away in cabinets and closets here. I thought there would be something powerful and even kind of zen about working in a house where another artist had lived and died, but maybe I was wrong. Maybe it's cursed."

Richard laughed, and he sounded just like his sister. "Curses aren't real, Hesper."

"Something feels unfinished here. The boy in the paintings—it's like he's waiting for something. I don't know if I want to be here when it arrives."

"It's not like you to be so unnerved. Maybe you should paint over them."

Hesper shuddered. "Definitely not. That would be an act of violence. I can't destroy someone else's work. It's not as if these are sidewalk chalk drawings or something. If they were hanging in a gallery instead of our kitchen, they'd be the darling of critics. They're fantastic. They're just...frightening, somehow."

Richard pulled her to her feet and stood with her, framing her cheeks in his hands as he pressed a kiss to her forehead. "This move has unsettled you, that's all. Once you can get your wheel running, you'll forget all about this. You'll forget about me."

"Never!"

"Always," Richard corrected her, his voice sad though his lips smiled. "The clay's your first love, and we both know it."

A horn honked, and Hesper's eyes flew to the window against which Richard's desk stood. A white van emblazoned with a sparkly logo was bouncing up the drive. "Thank goodness. The electrician is here."

Hastily Hesper padded down the hall to the open front

door. A man with salt-and-pepper hair and a trim goatee was climbing down from the driver's seat. He came to greet her with a broad smile.

"Ms. Dunn?"

"That's me. I'm so glad to see you. I was worried you might get lost."

"Oh, no. I know all these back roads. And I rigged this place up the last time. Shouldn't take me too long. I'm Roger, Roger Bernard. Gloria said you have new solar panels here somewhere?"

Gloria Padilla was the realtor. Hesper had all but forgotten the woman's name.

"Yes."

Hesper led the way to the shed and unlocked the door, propping it open. "My husband and I don't know anything about electricity, I'm afraid, so I'll have to leave everything up to you. The only thing I do know is that my kiln will need a dedicated system. I'm guessing everything else you can just set up the way it was before?"

Roger smiled at her reassuringly. "Should be no problem. Want to show me where your kiln will be?"

It was always a little dicey as a woman, especially in such a remote location, having strange men out to work her property, so she was relieved Roger seemed like a decent professional focused on his task. He didn't give off a single creepy vibe, thank goodness. Hesper supposed Gloria was probably sensitive to such things and wouldn't have recommended him otherwise. Hesper showed him around and explained what she needed for her kiln and then headed back to finish unpacking.

Having someone else around grounded her somehow. The paintings trapped in the doors—she couldn't help thinking of them that way—no longer struck her as eerie. They were sad, really. All that beautiful talent and skill hidden away in the darkness, as their creator was hidden away in the darkness of the earth. Assuming he was buried. Maybe he'd been cremated.

That was a nicer thought, Hesper decided. She liked the idea of being set adrift on a searing desert wind, blowing through the arroyos and singing across hoodoos and hidden canyons.

Now that she was done being melodramatic, it took no time at all to unload her few kitchen items into the cabinets. Her cooking repertoire was fairly simple. If she wanted something fancy to eat, she'd rather go to a restaurant. Richard wasn't that picky, either. And given that at least half her recipes were some variation on Mexican food, Hesper figured she'd moved to the right place. If nothing else, her green chili skills would surely improve.

She still needed to make a grocery store run and fill these cabinets with something besides empty dishes. She had enough pizza and breadsticks left over to survive the night, but tomorrow would be a town day.

Besides, she wanted to stop by the real estate office and have a conversation with Gloria what's-her-name. She clearly hadn't asked enough questions earlier. If nothing else, she needed to know the name of the little boy who was apparently her housemate now. She didn't have the slightest doubt that he was a real, specific child. There was nothing of the virtual about those eyes.

The benefit of living small was ease of moving, Hesper concluded contentedly three hours later. Her bookshelves were full, her closet hung. She'd set up her electric wheel in the spare bedroom where she'd dragged Richard's desk that morning. Tubs of clay lined the walls in front of more shelves that held the few pieces she'd brought with her.

She cared for her business side of art as much as she cared for interior decorating. Waste of life, she was sure. So while many other artists she knew maintained bustling online stores, she held to old-school patterns, working exclusively through local galleries and the occasional art market. Most of her finished work remained in galleries in Evanston and Chicago. She'd need to forge new relationships with the shops here.

That would be no mean feat. She'd basically moved to the art center of the country. Galleries here could be as selective as they liked, choosing from the very best of the best. Not to mention that most customers who came to Santa Fe to purchase pieces wanted the world-class Native American art the region was famous for. Hesper hoped to learn from those communities, but she couldn't claim any connection herself. If anything, she was perhaps a somewhat Scandinavian mutt, and her own style had been influenced primarily by those legacies. Up to now, anyway.

A frisson of anxiety crept up her spine. She'd promised herself this would be an immersive time, a season of learning and listening. She'd once loved being a student, happily devoting herself to sitting at the feet of any potter who would humor her, absorbing their philosophy and style and approach. She'd learned more through those relationships than in any college classroom. But since the accident, an odd reluctance to re-enter life had seized her fast.

Trips to the grocery store became major expeditions. Ginny was the only phone call she'd take without screening. She'd turned down invitations to every First Friday and gallery opening for the last four months. In crowds, her breath came fast and shallow. It was as if she possessed a horror of life itself, dreading every step forward.

No wonder Ginny had feared this move was a step toward hermitage. Reclusivity, Ginny had insisted, was a common response to trauma, but not a healthy one.

"You have to resist. You've got to fight to stay here, in this world, when you don't want to anymore."

"This is me fighting," Hesper had told her. "I need this."

Ginny had finally relented, or at least resigned herself to what she couldn't change.

Now that she was here, Hesper already felt as if chains clung to her ankles. The reluctance to leave the house sank into her bones like lethargy. It was just as well she hadn't stopped for groceries on the way here, or it might be weeks before she persuaded herself to leave, she thought wryly.

Tomorrow, she told herself firmly. Tomorrow, you have to buy groceries, and go to the real estate office.

Or at least call. Sure. She could call Gloria instead. After all, she could charge her battery tonight now that the electricity would be working. But she would definitely go to the grocery store. And she could drive up and down the streets to get names of galleries she could look up and contact online.

She could do that. It wasn't as if she was agoraphobic or anything, after all. She was simply tired. Didn't have much reserves left for dealing with other people and all their neediness.

She jumped nearly out of her skin when Roger knocked on the door of the bedroom.

"Ms. Dunn? I'm all done here. Why don't I show you and your husband how everything works and see if you have any questions?"

"Oh, sure," she said, getting hastily to her feet. "Don't worry about Richard. You can just show me."

He started in the house, going room by room, and ended by explaining how the battery array worked out in the shed. She was signing off on his clipboard when they heard another vehicle approaching. Hesper squinted down the road. A big brown van. Ginny's package must be arriving a day earlier than she expected.

"Thank you so much, Mr. Bernard," she said. "I'll call if I have any questions."

"Are you sure you don't want me to explain this to your husband, too?" He had the funniest expression on his face. Hesper couldn't make it out. Patriarchy, she decided cavalierly.

"Oh, no." She fluttered a hand back toward the house. "He doesn't have any more a head for that sort of thing than I do. If I'm honest, we'll probably just call you if we have any trouble. We're not the handiest people."

He smiled weakly. "Well, take care of yourself, Ms. Dunn. It can get lonely out here."

Why did people keep assuming she would be lonely? Her gaze narrowed.

"You said you set this system up last time. Did you know the artist who lived here before me?"

He shifted on his feet. "I didn't know him, exactly. Just met him the once. A nice guy. It was a shame what happened to him."

Funny turn of phrase, thought Hesper. Like some

quirk of fate, rather than an act of will. She knew what devastation quirks of fate could wreak. But that wasn't what had happened in this place.

"I'm not in any danger here," she said, although she couldn't have explained the impulse to reassure this stranger.

"I hope not," he responded cryptically. "Maybe I'll see you around town. Try not to get buried out here."

The delivery van rumbled up to a stop at that moment, and Roger Bernard disappeared into his own vehicle with a hasty wave. A cloud of dust, and he was gone.

Hesper shook her head. He'd seemed so normal right up until the end. Superstition got the best of most people at some point, she supposed. And from what she'd read, lots of the folks in these parts had pretty strong feelings about the places of the dead. She should probably count herself lucky he'd been willing to come out at all.

The delivery driver was there and gone so quickly, she wasn't sure if they'd even been a man or woman. The sun was a fiery pool on the horizon, and she was alone with yet another box to be unpacked.

That struck her funny.

"Thanks a lot, Ginny," she said as she carried it into the house.

CHAPTER THREE

"Well, these are...interesting."

A collection of five tapestry-style wall hangings, each about a foot and a half square, had been in the box. Hesper had them laid out on her recliner where she could survey them. Outside, the sun had all but slipped away, and the shadows in the living room were long and deep. Already the air cooled, for which Hesper was enormously thankful.

Unicorns?

While it was true much of Hesper's art drew its inspiration from mythology, she tended to be drawn to darker, earthier images. Jormungand or fertility goddesses. Not unicorns and rainbows and princesses with long golden hair. What in the world had Ginny been thinking?

Hesper couldn't deny there was something rather hypnotic about the panels. A sea of flowers and tiny animals formed the backdrop for what appeared to be an islanded garden where the story itself was told. Because this had to be a story, didn't it? The same characters appeared repeatedly, though their poses and expressions differed from image to image. A lion, a unicorn, a lady. Sometimes a smaller woman, who must be a lady-in-waiting. All set within the confines of a wooded garden.

Confines. Maybe that was what Ginny wanted her to see? That an oasis could become a prison? The innumerable blossoms painstakingly stitched into the wool filled the panels corner to corner, and myriad little creatures romped everywhere without regard for the garden's boundaries. But the lady, the lion, and the unicorn appeared to be trapped in their paradise.

Hesper shook her head. No sense woolgathering over this. She'd call Ginny tomorrow and find out what it was all about. No doubt there was some elaborate interpretation. She snickered. She loved Ginny, but the woman couldn't help being outrageously pretentious sometimes.

It was an hour later in Illinois, though, and Ginny was an early riser. Besides, Hesper didn't feel up to a conversation just now. Of course, tomorrow would probably be worse. She'd have had to navigate a grocery store and had her difficult conversation with Gloria, too. But hey. Maybe it would be better to get it all over with at once. Yeah. A one-and-done.

The familiar longing to slide beneath the covers in bed and not come back out eked under her skin. To sink into the darkness and warmth until that darkness and warmth consumed her. Maybe it had already. Maybe she lay in bed, now, back in the Evanston apartment, and this was all a dream. Maybe soon all her cells and sensations and intentions would dissipate into nothingness. Maybe peace was very, very near.

No. She knew better. Dying easy of a broken heart was a

myth perpetrated by bad poetry. And she'd never been a student of verse.

The solar panels hadn't had enough time, so she'd just charge her phone in the car on the way to town tomorrow. It wasn't late, but she was beat after unpacking and moving furniture and tubs of clay all day. She used a package of wipes to take a truck-stop bath before grabbing a bottle of water and loading a plate with the last of the breadsticks. At least the bed was put together. The bedroom felt cozy, in spite of the dark.

Her space. Their space, hers and Richard's. A refuge.

She left the windows open. Why bother locking up out here in the middle of nowhere? And the cool night air was delicious. Once she had fans set up, it would be very comfortable, she was sure. The massive stucco walls acted almost as a refrigerant. Hopefully the reverse would be true come winter. The living room sported a wood stove, but she wasn't exactly a lumberjack. Oh, well. She'd no doubt fall off that bridge when she came to it.

She set up the flashlight like a lamp on the nightstand. Deliberately she forced her mind away from the thought of the little boy locked away in all her cabinets and closets. Surely he would be happy now that she'd pulled the paper away from his face. She was a benevolent visitor, not an enemy. Not an interloper. Wasn't she?

She laughed nervously, the sound rattling around her

and heightening her unease. What was wrong with her? They were paintings, for Pete's sake. Just paintings. Weird, but hardly otherworldly.

She snuggled down under the multi-colored wedding ring quilt, another gift from Ginny. The rhythm of Richard's breathing beside her, regular and dream-weighted, centered her. This was their new home. Their castle, as the unicorn-lady would probably say. Here only what they permitted would exist. Nothing could hurt them here. This world would be what they made it. No invasions from what other people imagined was the real world.

She snagged the new book Ginny had recommended from the nightstand where she'd unpacked it earlier. She'd come here to learn, after all. To hear what the desert had to say. Where better to start than by listening to the people who had befriended this place the longest? Thoroughly absorbed by the Navajo legends unfolding from the pages, she didn't even notice how stale the breadsticks had become.

Her bladder and her sadly crooked neck woke her from dreams of coyotes and ravens. The flashlight's beam had dimmed.

"Licorice sticks." She'd seen the battery charger around here somewhere yesterday, hadn't she? Surely the flashlight would last long enough to get her to the outhouse and back.

Habit had her reaching across the sheets before she slipped out of bed, but the other side was cold and empty.

Her heart shuddered.

"Focus," she told herself sternly. "Priorities. You need to pee."

She slid her feet into the espadrilles waiting beside the bed, remembering too late that she needed to get into the habit of shaking them out first. She didn't want to jam her toes into a sleepy scorpion or spider. But fate, so far, was on her side. No squishies.

Once outside, she snapped the flashlight off. Its pale beam was no match for the full moon light gleaming almost day-bright. She sighed with delight, all her trepidation fleeing. She raised her face to the silver moon, felt the cool night wind murmur against her skin like a late summer creek rippling over her bare toes. Insects sang an untroubled chorus from the wall of trees that stood refuge to the house. Long, blade-sharp shadows stretched from the base of their trunks.

This. This was why they'd come here. Peace. Beauty. Haven. The only sounds here were the sounds of life.

Once in the pitch-black of the outhouse, she tried flipping the flashlight back on to worry away any creeping spiders, but the thing had given up the ghost for good. "Son of a cinnamon stick," she grumbled, finishing up her business as quickly as she could.

The outhouse stood tucked under the trees. The dusty ground and scattered rocks outside the courtyard gleamed bone-white in the moonlight. Hesper gasped, clutching the flashlight like a weapon as she froze in place on shaky legs.

A boy, or the black silhouette of what looked like a boy, crouched by the courtyard wall, his attention focused on something on the ground. At Hesper's gasp, he raised his head. White light blazed from his eye sockets. He shot to his feet and dashed away, disappearing into the courtyard.

"Wait!" Hesper cried, running after him. Inside the gate, he was nowhere to be seen. Her kiln and pottery wheel, with her stool beside it, were all that stood on the wide flagstones. Where could he have gone?

With horror, her gaze went to the living room window and the front door that she'd left standing open behind her when she came outside. He had to have gone into the house. It was the only place to go. He hadn't been big enough to scale the walls.

He isn't big enough to be out here in the middle of nowhere by himself, either, her brain hissed. Stop. Think. What is happening here?

No way did she want to go back inside that dark house where God-knows-what waited for her without even a working flashlight to see what she was walking into. But what was the alternative? Spend the night out here, waiting for him to reappear? Or for whomever he was with to show themselves?

The nearest neighbor was at least ten miles away.

Anyone out here on her property had no good intentions. Maybe the boy was supposed to distract her. Or lure her. Maybe he'd gotten away from whomever he was with and wasn't part of any plot at all.

Those eyes. Hesper shivered. Was there such a thing as an abyss of light? It had surely only been the moonlight's reflection. Hadn't it?

Or maybe—Hesper swallowed. Maybe he wasn't there at all. Ginny had been worried about her before she left Evanston, Hesper knew. Worried that her imagination was running away with her. Stress, Ginny said. Stress and trauma could prompt the brain into all sorts of survival behaviors.

She never said crazy, but Hesper could see the fear in Ginny's compassionate smile.

She'd been extra tired when she went to bed. Hadn't she? Her mind full of those cabinet-door paintings and Navajo legends. And it was the middle of the night, after all. Maybe she wasn't as fully awake as she thought she was. Shadows could play tricks on the eyes at the best of times. She didn't really believe some lone child was here running around her house and playing in its rooms, did she?

No. Obviously not. She was psyching herself out, that was all.

A breeze lifted the hair off the back of her neck with light fingers. She'd thrown on one of Richard's button-down shirts when she got out of bed, and now she clutched it to her neck like some horrified Victorian matron. She tried and failed to summon a derisive smile at herself as she held the flashlight in front of her as a club and inched toward the blackness of the open front door.

She strained her ears, searching for the sound of anyone else's breathing, for footsteps on the hardwood floors, but all she could hear was her own heartbeat's frantic thudding. She eased inside, holding her breath. The dark swallowed her instantly. She longed to glance back, to reassure herself that the world still stood, to remember the perfect solace that had embraced her when she first stepped out there, but she daren't light-blind her eyes by looking back at the moonlight.

Now that she was inside, she could see scant outlines emerging. Her recliner. The dining room table. The hallway. She stood there for long minutes, her whole body straining to perceive something, anything, in the darkness that didn't belong.

But the house felt empty. Her own ragged breathing and the chorus of the crickets were all she heard.

Down that hallway. She only had to make it down the hallway and into her bedroom. Her pottery studio, with Richard's desk at the wide window, stood at the end. She'd closed that door earlier. The bathroom beside it would be closed, too. She just had to reach her bedroom. Then she could dive under the covers and escape this silly nightmare she'd created for herself out of compulsive thoughts and exhausted delusions.

One creeping step forward. Wait. Listen. Eyes opening wider and wider against the darkness.

Two steps forward. Three.

Hesper broke into a run, her shoes slapping on the floor, fear groaning its way out of her throat. She daren't look to see if the doors were closed as they ought to be. She flung herself into her bedroom and slammed the door shut behind her. She leaned against it, panting, willing her eyes to adjust faster to the dim moonlight pouring over the window lip.

"Richard?" she whispered hoarsely.

She could make out his shoulders hunched in the wooden chair she'd set in the corner. Why was he facing the wall? It looked as though he was cradling his head in his hands.

"Richard?"

Moonlight hallucinations forgotten, Hesper stepped forward. The chair spun to face her, impossibly fast. Richard's dead eyes stared at her accusingly from the horrible angle of a broken neck, his head cradled in his right hand. Blood streaked his pale skin.

"No!" Hesper howled. She rushed forward, falling to her knees before him, throwing herself around his legs in a desperate embrace. But her cheekbone smashed into the hard wooden seat of the chair, her arms clutching at empty air.

"Hesper!" came Richard's urgent voice from the bed. "Hesper, you're dreaming. You're dreaming again. Come back to bed, honey."

Relief shuddered through her, so powerful she nearly passed out. "Richard," she sobbed, dragging herself to the bed and crawling under the blankets. His strong arms wrapped tightly around her, drew her to his chest. As his heartbeat pounded, sure and steady, in her ear, her breathing slowed, her trembling eased.

"You were dead again," she whispered brokenly.

"Hush." His left hand combed the sweaty tangles of her hair. "It's just a dream. I'm here. I'm here."

She clung to his broad back.

CHAPTER FOUR

Before she left for the grocery store, Hesper walked around the perimeter of the courtyard. She felt silly, but it was still reassuring to see no footprints in the dust besides her own.

Richard and Ginny were right. She was overwrought. She grinned crookedly at herself. How very appropriately melodramatic for an artist, she thought cynically. Waking nightmares and compulsive thinking were symptoms that would surely go away once she could lose herself in the clay. Today would be the last of the moving details that required much of her attention. She still needed to schedule the satellite installation so she could have internet service, but that was simple enough.

Tomorrow, she promised herself. Tomorrow she would sit in the sun and listen to the wheel sing and see what stories the clay had to tell. Tomorrow she would start to heal.

She loaded the trash into the back of the Subaru and waved toward Richard's desk before driving away. No trash service out here, unsurprisingly. Maybe this would be the push she needed to seriously reduce her waste impact. That wouldn't be a bad thing.

"You are my sunshine, my only sunshine," she hummed absently to herself as the desert spun away under her tires. Sweeping mesas and stony outcroppings filled her gaze, the fierce blue sky competing for her attention with casino billboards. An unexpected hopefulness lodged in her chest.

It lasted until she reached the grocery store parking lot. "Mastodon-muncher," she said weakly as the old dread crept back over her.

It took fifteen minutes of watching people mill in and out of the automatic doors, wrestling carts and juggling purchases, before she managed to force herself to retrieve her reusable bags from the back seat and go inside.

"Face your fears," she ordered in her best imitation of Ginny as she forced herself to make eye contact as she passed people, to smile and nod and murmur hello. Reach for the apple, for the box of pasta, for the paper towels.

Long-term reward over short-term gratification, she thought. As much as she wanted to get out of this place, away from the garish lights and glaring strangers and mishmash of colors and labels and screaming boxes, she needed to get a full load of supplies. The better she did this time, the longer respite before she had to come back. And she needed all the basics—rice and flour and dry goods. Coffee.

In an effort to fool her brain into thinking it was all one stop, she pushed her wheezing grocery cart into the liquor store next door rather than unloading her bags into the car first. A case of ciders, a case of beer, some Fireball and Sailor Jerry's, and she was good to go. She even managed some small talk she promptly forgot with the clerk. Had it been a man or a woman? Maybe neither. She wasn't sure.

Back behind the wheel, Hesper stretched her arms, rolled her neck. She'd done well, hadn't she? What had felt insurmountable this morning was now already accomplished. She'd disposed of the trash on the way in, and now her car was loaded with all the goods she would need for at least two weeks, maybe three or four if she stretched it. She'd been nice to strangers and hadn't cried for no reason even once. She was a mastodon-munching rockstar.

On a whim, she opened the maps app on her phone. She whistled as she pulled out of her parking spot. She wasn't going to call Gloria. She'd drop by the office, like any normal person would be able to do, no problem. Likely the realtor would be more inclined to share information in person, right? Hesper would be personable. Charming. She'd be irresistible. Gloria would spill all she knew.

Why exactly did all realtors look like they just left a Glamour Shots photoshoot? Hesper wondered fifteen minutes later, as she sat across from Gloria Padilla (*Padilla, Padilla, why couldn't she remember that?*) in a sidewalk corner office. All Hesper's intended charm evaporated in an inhale of hairspray and gardenia perfume. She was going to suffocate in this place. Choking to death on plastic air.

"It's so wonderful to finally meet you in person," Gloria gushed through red-plastered lips. "Isn't that the most fantastic little enclave out there? It's like it was built specifically for an artist."

"Yes, it's everything I'd hoped for—" Hesper began, but Gloria rattled on.

"Oh!" She rummaged in her desk drawers. "I'm so glad you dropped by. I meant to leave this for you in the kitchen to have when you arrived, but I forgot."

Hesper peered into the gift bag Gloria handed her. A bottle of pink Cupcake wine, a plastic clamshell filled with what Hesper couldn't deny were amazing-looking cupcakes, and a Mariah Carey Christmas CD. Hesper choked back a laugh.

"Thank you. You didn't need to do this." Really.

"Oh, I want all my clients to feel like family. Just because the sale is over, doesn't mean our relationship is. I'm here to help you settle into your new community any way I can. So, what can I do for you? You must have had some reason to drop by? No trouble, I hope?"

Was that real anxiety darkening Gloria's mascara-draped eyes? Or something darker, something more like fear? Hesper pushed the notion away.

"Nothing wrong," she reassured the other woman with what she hoped was a warm smile, even if it felt like fishing line was drawing back the corners of her lips. "I just find myself more curious than I thought I'd be about the previous owner, and I was hoping you wouldn't mind indulging me a bit."

Yes, Gloria's smile was definitely strained now.

"Someone has pasted up shelf paper over the inside of all the cabinet and closet doors. When I pulled them down, I found some truly fantastic paintings, gallery-class work, but they were all of the same boy. And all hidden, of course. Do you happen to know the significance of that boy to the artist who was there before me? And what was the artist's name, anyway? I should have asked earlier. It might even be someone I'm familiar with."

Gloria's smile clung stubbornly to her powdered face. "I'm sure you haven't heard of him."

"I quite like the paintings." That was true, wasn't it? They were certainly very compelling. "I'd like to understand them better. One artist to another, you know."

More often than not, people would excuse any eccentricity once she attached the word "art." Hesper wondered how other people explained away their quirks without such a convenient crutch. It must be very difficult.

"His name was Leon Oberman."

Hesper's eyes widened in surprise even as Gloria's filled with what appeared to be genuine tears. Hesper *did* know Leon Oberman. Not personally, but by reputation. His work was highly sought after, but he wasn't known as a prolific artist. It was hard to reconcile the dozens of his pieces hiding in her house with his career. And she had heard something a while back about his untimely death, but she couldn't recall any details, if she'd ever known any.

"He really was the nicest man. People talk about artists like that as if they're difficult—oh, I'm so sorry, I don't mean that across the board, I just mean other people, you know, other artists." Gloria's hands fluttered. "But he wasn't like that at all. He was kind. I never guessed what would happen."

Hesper struggled to detangle Gloria's threads of thought.

"The boy, of course. That was his son. Leon was a single dad, and his son—well, you can probably tell from the portraits. Down's Syndrome, you know. Poor little babies. He died. Pneumonia, I think. Something like that. Leon never recovered."

Something cold and oddly familiar settled in Hesper's belly. "So, Leon came out to the desert to start over?"

Gloria dabbed at her eyes with a tissue. Hesper had to hand it to her—not a streak of makeup marred her face.

"Yes. And I think he really was happy for a while. I'm sure of it. I used to see him at the bakery sometimes. He always smiled at me. Sometimes people get overwhelmed in a moment, you know? I'm sure he didn't really mean to do it."

Hesper nodded understandingly. Inwardly she considered how bizarre the measurements by which other people's happiness was gauged. Leon Oberman must have been able to find happiness after the death of his young son because he smiled at a realtor when he saw her in the bakery?

People mystified her.

51

"I'm so sorry to have upset you," she said. "But thank you for sharing his story. That helps me. And I imagine it would have been important to him that people would know and remember his son. Otherwise, he wouldn't have created so many paintings of him."

Although that didn't really mesh with closing them all up in dark cabinets and rooms where no one could see them. Hesper didn't think Gloria would examine her words that deeply, though.

Sure enough, the other woman cheered slightly, like a morning-glory perking up under the sun. She wasn't a bad sort, Hesper decided. It probably wasn't even her fault she was so plastic. Basic qualification for a woman in a face-forward occupation. Hesper wished she'd felt more generous and less derisive when she'd come into the office. Oh, well. She wasn't exactly unfamiliar with her own personal failings.

"One other question." Hesper remembered as she rose to her feet and collected her purse. "I guess I need to buy a new bathroom mirror. There's only an empty frame hanging over the sink. Is there...?"

Without warning, the woman dissolved wholesale into tears, mascara be damned. *Be bojangled*, Hesper's brain automatically corrected her.

"That's how it happened," Gloria managed. "That's how he did it."

"With a mirror?"

"He broke the mirror and stabbed himself in the neck with a shard of glass."

"Oh, ham sandwiches."

"What?" Gloria looked up at her, confused.

"I'm so sorry," Hesper said again. "That is awful. I had no idea." She seized a handful of tissues from the box on the desk and thrust them at Gloria.

Gloria rummaged in another drawer, pulling herself back together with a visible effort. "Here you are." She handed Hesper a business card. "Best prices in town on glass. Good people."

She stood, pulling herself up to her full if diminutive height and holding out her hand in a clear dismissal. Hesper shook it.

"Do call again if there is anything else I can do. It was lovely to meet you in person."

Hesper collected her gift bag and beat a hasty retreat. She pulled away from the office as soon as she slid into the driver's seat, not wanting to make poor Gloria pretend to look busy and unaffected in the big picture window.

Stabbed himself in the neck with a shard of the mirror? Son of a cinnamon stick, that was mastodon-munching *grim*. Hesper had never heard of anything like it. Didn't men usually shoot or hang themselves? Or even retreat to the tired old standard of drinking one's self to death? She had to agree with Gloria that Leon Oberman couldn't possibly had thought that out in advance. It must've been an act of terrible desperation.

Hesper pictured Leon Oberman wandering the house alone, with his son's face confronting him everywhere he turned. Again she wondered if the act of hiding them away in the cupboards had been an effort to escape his ghosts, or if it had been the last futile attempt of a father to keep safe the son he couldn't protect in real life.

So terribly sad.

On the drive home, she resolved not to tell Richard what she'd learned. This place was their new start. She wouldn't stain their threshold with the shadows of old ghosts.

Together she and Richard would breathe new life into the hacienda. It would be a place of love and creation. An oasis whose springs welled first in their hearts.

CHAPTER FIVE

"Okay, you got some 'splainin' to do," Hesper told Ginny in her best Ricky Ricardo. The cell, fully charged, was on speaker phone, sitting on the kitchen counter while Hesper found homes for all her groceries. She took a ridiculous delight in the refrigerator that was already beginning to cool. She couldn't explain how she took pride in the sun's ability to power her little commune here, but she puffed up happily nonetheless.

Ginny laughed, knowing full well what Hesper referred to. "Okay, stay with me. It's a little complicated, but I think it will resonate with you in the end. And there's even a six-hundred-year-old mystery—maybe you'll be the one to solve it."

"Well, you know I'm a devout fan of Psych and Miss Marple, so if anyone is qualified to solve a mystery, it's got to be me."

"All right, here goes. So this series of tapestries, rather unoriginally called *The Lady and the Unicorn*, was commissioned back at the turn of the sixteenth century. I know you know from all your fine arts classes how absolutely soaked the art of the Middle Ages was in symbolism. You could probably stare at any one of those pieces for years and still not find all the allusions in the stitching.

"But the basic conclusion scholars have arrived at is that

each of the panels represents the Lady's relationship with each of the five senses. Folks have argued about the order of the panels, but there is a cheat: if you count the number of sigils shown on each panel, an order is revealed, numbered one to five. Sight, Hearing, Touch, Taste, and Smell."

Hesper stretched her neck out to cast a critical glance over the panels heaped on her recliner.

"Umm...there's six panels."

"Yes!" Ginny sounded delighted. Hesper couldn't help smiling. Her sister-in-law was such a hopeless nerd. Counting to six was not much of an accomplishment, was it?

"That's where the mystery comes in. The sixth panel is the only one with a written clue to its meaning. The tent behind the Lady is emblazoned with the words 'A Mon Seul Desir.' That could mean *to my heart's only desire* or *by my will alone.* As far as the image goes, the Lady is either taking off or putting on the elaborate necklace she's worn in all the other panels. And there's a repeat in the number of sigils. Instead of six sigils, there are three again."

"Ah, mysterious indeed. Three sigils."

"Don't mock! People at the time were fascinated by the conflict between the flesh and the spirit. Even so, it's highly unusual to have that conflict explored by a woman—the lady— without the presence or influence of any men or divine images, like angels or knights or priests. And what is she choosing? Is she turning away from the sensual world

CASSONDRA WINDWALKER

and adopting a monastic life? Or is she terribly modern and actually abandoning her status to pursue her own will, whatever that is? And the presence of the lion and the unicorn, how they react to her behavior in each panel, is so curious. Are they guardians? Guides? Fellow hedonists?"

"And I'm supposed to figure that out?" Hesper snorted. "I'm not exactly a medieval arts scholar, you know, Ginny."

"Maybe you and the Lady have more in common than you think. You're exploring what you want, too. Making decisions about what to hold onto and what to leave behind." Hesper worked faster, sorting cans, as Ginny paused, swallowing. "Maybe you'll be the one to discover what her one desire really was."

Hesper forced a chuckle over the lump in her throat. "Okay, I'm starting to see the connections. As usual, you give the most thoughtful gifts. And, actually, even though the style is wildly different from the rest of the house, the colors will be quite striking once I hang them."

"Oh?'

"Yeah, the walls are that ruddy stucco orange, so the vivid reds and blues and greens of the wool will brighten the place up. And it's not as if the rest of my art collection has any consistent aesthetic, anyway. I'm nothing if not eclectic."

"You've never been inclined to easy labels. Or easy anything." Tactfully Ginny changed topics. "How are things

57

coming together? Do you have electricity yet?"

"Yep! I'm a fully functioning little power station now. I still can't waste electricity like a profligate, of course, but I'm pretty excited about a real shower tonight. And I'll get internet access soon. For now, I can use my phone to check email and anything urgent. You know, if some gallery in Chicago makes me a millionaire while I'm not looking."

"As is fated to happen eventually."

Hesper's smile lingered after she told her sister-in-law goodbye. Maybe Ginny and Felka would come visit her soon. While New Mexico might hold almost nothing in common with northern Illinois, the regions did share an incredible wealth of history and museums and communion with the past. And given that Felka had somehow weirdly managed to cling to her Catholic faith in spite of its rejection of her and her marriage, Hesper thought Felka would enjoy visiting the many cathedrals and missions of the area. The Catholic relationship with the native peoples of what was now New Mexico was similarly as dark and complicated as its relationship with gay or nonbinary people.

It was remarkable how some people possessed such limitless capacity for tolerance and compassion while others apparently possessed none at all. Hesper and Ginny tended to just smile and nod whenever Felka referred to her faith. Neither of them wanted to take it away from her, however little they understood its persistence. Hesper sighed.

But now—food! Real food.

Hesper tossed some ramen noodles in a pan with hot sauce, soy sauce, and a can of water chestnuts. Richard might take issue with her definition of real food, but she'd never been one to spend hours in a kitchen. Food went in and went out. She'd rather spend what few minutes she had making things that couldn't be flushed away. (The vast number of pottery finds at archeological digs centered on public toilets notwithstanding.) And as far as she was concerned, this was every bit as tasty as something slaved over with a raised pinkie and a French accent.

She should probably call and schedule an appointment with the satellite company, but hadn't she peopled enough for one day? And she was in no hurry to re-enter the virtual world, anyway. She had a sadly neglected Instagram where she posted pictures of her new pieces as she completed them. She'd dropped Facebook after the accident. Too many people she barely knew, all wanting to lay claim to her loss and compete with each other for most flowery condolences. And she'd never figured out the point of Twitter, though she thought she remembered one of the gallery owners helping her set up an account at some point. Hopefully some robot hadn't stolen her password and commenced with posting weird political stuff in her name by now.

Maybe the new world, the present world, was racing away from her. She was still a few months from thirty, but she felt like a crone. Or maybe this world, with its unforgiving sun and dusty winds and rich clay hiding beside secret springs, was the only real after all.

Richard was real, and that was enough. If there was a world where he wasn't, she didn't want to draw a single breath of its air.

A near-panic overtook her at the thought, and she flew down the hall, barely pausing to knock before she flung open the studio door. Her heart slammed happily in her chest at the sight of him there, his dark head bent over his papers like always. He twisted in his chair to face her with an indulgent smile.

"Thinking too much again, darling?"

"Always," she confessed as he stood and drew her close.

"You should come see the presents your silly sister sent us. I'm going to hang them up in the living room."

"Them? Please tell me my sister isn't taking over our decorating." Ginny and Felka did have a particular fondness for traditional Polish furniture and dishes that Richard and Hesper did not share.

"It's a set of small tapestries. I think you'll actually like them. They tell a story of some sort. *The Lady and the Unicorn*. Ginny said she thinks I'm the Lady, so I guess that makes you the unicorn?"

"Well, I am endowed with a substantial horn, so that works."

Hesper boxed his arm.

"Ow! What? I thought you were fond of horns."

"You are totally ruining the symbolism of the pieces with your dirty mind."

"I doubt that. That whole mythology about capturing unicorns by persuading them to lay their heads down in a virgin's lap in the middle of the woods? You couldn't get more obvious if you tried. If anything, I'm the personification of its intent. Me and my immense manliness."

Hesper laughed. "I guess you're right. We tend to assign a veneer of respectable prudery to anything old, but people have always been primal. We just dress up our hungers in different costumes."

"Exactly. Now why don't you show me these new and bawdy additions to our home?"

Hesper took one of Richard's hands in both of hers and led him into the living room.

"I'm going to get a hammer and some nails. They have little ribbons for hanging."

She hung them on the blank interior wall facing the recliner in a sort of pyramid, Sight at the top, Hearing and Touch in the second row, with Taste, Smell, and A Mon Seul Desir forming the foundation. Richard lounged in the recliner and looked on with a debauched eye.

"The color does add a nice energy," Richard approved,

tilting his head as he examined the images. Hesper summarized what Ginny had explained about the supposed import of each piece.

"Hmm. So are you going to be the one to unravel this mystery—pun intended, of course?"

"That seems unlikely. But I have to admit, the more I stare at them, the more intriguing they are. There's so much going on. And the expressions, of the women and of the animals, don't fit neatly into some category of commonly interpreted medieval thought. I kind of like them."

"Good." Richard wrapped his arms around her from behind and nuzzled her neck under her hair.

"Stop that," she swatted at him, "I smell like baby wipes and sweat. I don't remember the last time I had a real shower."

"You should rectify that. And hey—no midnight treks to the outhouse anymore. That's a good thing. We are fully modern again."

"An excellent thing."

Unbidden, a vision of the shadow-boy rose to her mind. She shivered and shot an uneasy glance around the room.

Richard's hands gripped her shoulders. "Seeing things, honey?"

"I was a little worked up last night. Tired and disturbed by all those paintings. Sometimes my imagination just runs away with me. You know that."

"Have you been taking your medication?"

He knew better than to ask that. She spun away from under his hold, anger sparking. "I'm going to clean up. Don't expect me to re-emerge for at least an hour."

She made it an affair. She lit a sage and lavender candle and set it on the sink. She tossed one of those aromatherapy bombs in the floor of the shower and drenched herself happily in curtains of hot water. She used the pads of her fingers to massage her scalp, sudsing her long hair luxuriantly. She shaved her legs with a new razor, delighting in each smooth, silky stroke along her muscled calves.

Thick, fluffy towels wrapped her in decadent warmth when she stepped out. She needed to string up a clothesline. Dryers used a lot of energy. There was a stackable unit in the linen closet in the hallway, but it didn't look as if it had ever seen much use. Hesper suspected Gloria had bought the units to add to the house's marketability. She supposed she could use it in a pinch, but it would be better to rely mostly on natural drying.

She flipped her head upside down and scrubbed her hair as dry as she could. She should do something with herself. A months-old chestnut dye job was fading out of her dirty blond hair. Richard called it honey-blond, but she knew better. It could hardly be described as any one color at all. She hadn't been to a salon for at least six months. Rather than attempt to butcher her own bangs, she'd let them grow out. Maybe she could do a copper-and-gold. Santa Fe surely had any number of excellent stylists.

As she flipped back her hair, she glanced assessingly into the blank wooden square where a mirror should've been.

She screamed.

CHAPTER SIX

A dark-haired man with hollow, scruffy cheeks, and night-black eyes stared back at Hesper. Sadness, terrible, terrible sadness, swamped her, and her knees buckled. She clutched at the edge of the sink. Leon Oberman—she knew unquestioningly it was he—held out a bloodied shard of glass to her. Her gaze jerked to his neck, but no wound bloomed there.

Could she stop him? If she seized the broken mirror from his hand, could she affect the past? Save him from himself? Clinging to the counter with her left hand, she reached out with shaking fingers.

"Hesper!"

Richard's voice sounded hoarsely behind her. She turned, and when she looked back, only the wooden panel and empty frame stared back at her.

Richard seized her right hand, uncurling her fingers. She stared uncomprehendingly at the blood dripping from her palm.

"Hesper, what did you do?" He jerked the faucet handle open and rinsed the stinging cut beneath the cool flow, wrapping it in a rag that immediately flowered pink and red. "God only knows where the bandages are. That's what I get for letting you do the organizing."

He seized the empty frame and flung it open. Hesper

flinched as Leon Oberman's son looked down soberly at her, wet and naked and blood-stained as she was. She thought of the night Leon Oberman ended his life. Had he stood right here, gazing at the broken mirror, his son forever on the other side of a door Leon finally figured out how to open?

"Here." Richard grabbed a box of Band-Aids and a bottle of hydrogen peroxide. She hardly noticed as he doused and rewrapped her hand.

Richard looked around, his gaze lighting on the razor lying on the floor of the shower. He grabbed it up, examining the blade before rinsing it off. "You've got to be more careful. We're not exactly close to a hospital. And who knows how long it would take for an ambulance to get here."

His eyes danced away from the painting as he fastened the cabinet door closed again. "Did you ever figure out what the deal is with those paintings, by the way? They're mastodon-munching creepy."

She gave a watery giggle, ignoring her stinging palm. "They are, aren't they? Just the eccentricity of the artist who lived here last, I gather." She hadn't told Richard the previous owner died on the premises. He didn't need to know something so dark. "The little boy was his son."

"Huh. Is it just me, or is there something ever so slightly unhealthy about locking your own son away on the other side of every door in the house?"

"Can't argue with that." She kept her tone deliberately

light. Hesper pulled on her nubbly violet robe and tied it around her waist, slipped her feet into a fuzzy pair of incongruous reindeer and Christmas cane socks. Richard raised his eyebrows but didn't comment on her choice.

"Maybe we should paint over them."

Black fury hit the back of Hesper's eyes like a sledgehammer.

"No."

Richard backed away, hands up, at her flat tone. "All right, all right. Just an idea."

"They're masterpieces. Destroying them would be some kind of sacrilege." Hesper swallowed the unexpected rage, willed herself to calm down. Richard scooped up her dirty clothes and led the way out of the bathroom. Guilt struck her when she noticed how careful, how controlled, his movements were. As if he feared to unbalance her, even by something so slight as an untempered motion.

"Maybe they should be in a gallery somewhere. A collection of doors like this would be pretty striking. I've certainly never seen anything like it in a museum."

"No. They belong here." Was that right? Didn't art belong more to the viewer than to the originator? Hesper rubbed her eyes, feeling confused. Tired.

"Okay. They stay here. Ham sandwiches, though, Hesper. You have to quit scaring me like this. Be more careful, okay?"

"Yes, sir."

I'm my own ghost, Hesper told herself as sternly as she could. She hadn't seen that shadow-boy until after she'd discovered all the paintings. Leon Oberman's horrifying wraith hadn't appeared till after Gloria Padilla had told his story. Her imagination was working overtime, fabricating images to match what she'd uncovered. Probably some clumsy attempt to distract herself from her own story. Pathetic, really.

She refused to be afraid of her dream house. This place was everything an artist could hope for. Remote, lovely, self-sufficient. Tied to the earth, with its clay walls and timber beams and stone flags. Evocative of the past, with inset tile images reflecting the aesthetic of the native peoples who had lived here for thousands of years. Here, she felt connected to the past and the future as if there were little difference between them, after all.

Contrary to what some people assumed, the desert was a place of incredible, irrepressible life. Tonight, as every night, when darkness fell, the wind rose, fierce and strong and brief in its sudden sweet relief from the crushing heat of the day. All that had lain in abeyance through the long hours of light rose: owls and foxes and coyotes and bats and dragonflies, sand-colored rodents and night-colored boys.

Stop that. She was done making up nightmares.

In the living room, she stood under the tapestries Ginny

had sent and fingered the fringe of the one at the very top.

"You like them" Richard said. He leaned against the wall by the dark fireplace, watching her, his hands in his pockets, his hair falling over his glasses like always. Hesper's gaze lingered a moment on the little round belly that made him self-conscious. She loved him so much.

"I do," she said, her voice tinged with surprise. "There's something kind of hypnotic about them. Almost disorienting, the longer I stare at them. So much is happening that I can almost, almost, but not quite see. I keep looking deeper in."

"Well, don't get lost."

"I won't. Or maybe I will, just for a little bit. Ginny may be on to something. These might be useful to me. To my own art. It's not as if we're grappling with anything different in the human experience from what they grappled with a thousand years ago. And here we are, living in a place that's been continuously occupied for much, much longer than that. It's all connected, somehow. Maybe what I need to be doing is finding that connection."

"That's why you're the artist, I suppose, and I'm the teacher."

Hesper hardly heard him, lost in her examination of the panel.

Staring into the background of the tapestry was like staring at the night sky: the longer she looked, the deeper she hurtled. She couldn't imagine the skill and vision it had required to weave the hundreds of unique flowers and animals, each with their own distinct expressions and poses, especially on the grand scale at which these tapestries were originally designed. She wished she remembered more of what she'd learned in school about the symbolism of the Middle Ages. Artists of that period had delighted in layers and layers of meaning, choosing every petal and flower with an eye to some more elaborate significance.

Some things she recalled. Dogs represented loyalty, rabbits fertility. *Obviously.* She grinned. Lions were always beasts of war, which was interesting since none of these panels alluded to battle, unless you counted the waving banners. No knights, no horses, no flashing blades. No men at all, not even a warning angel to keep this independent female to the straight and narrow. This Lady enjoyed a freedom none of the women of her period would have found familiar. Or maybe not. She was confined to her lovely garden, after all. Maybe she was in a prison.

The Unicorn itself was undoubtedly the most complex symbol. Savage and fierce and unspeakably swift, it patently stood for purity and innocence. But nobody could deny the powerful phallic implications of that horn. The Unicorn was freedom unassailable. Hesper knew that at the time of the tapestry's original weaving, the Unicorn wasn't considered a mythical creature but a real animal. Rarely sighted not because of some sorcery, but because its speed and cunning made it all but impossible to capture.

Except, of course, by the allure of a virgin, which this Lady was clearly meant to be.

Hesper had her doubts, though. It was funny—this panel was supposed to represent Sight, plainly enough with the inclusion of the mirror the Lady held up to the Unicorn's view. But to Hesper's eye, this image was heavy with all sorts of sensual implications.

For a virgin, the Lady didn't seem too intent on guarding her virtue. Though her hair remained demurely bound, her legs were splayed beneath the heavy weight of the Unicorn's forelegs. Her overskirt was hitched up, her underskirt transparent. She held up a hand mirror, as if to confront the Unicorn with some inner reality, but it was no use. Instead of becoming distracted by his own image like some narcissus, the Unicorn gazed gladly on her face, as if she alone held the answers he sought.

The Lion looked disdainfully away from the tableau, as if in contempt for the whole affair. Hesper found herself transfixed by the Lady's expression. No triumph or glee over her capture. Rather, she looked sad, somber, almost hopeless.

What had she hoped to achieve by trapping the Unicorn? In what lay her dismay? Was she sorry for her own deceit? Was she sad to have been used by hunstmen to destroy such a beautiful creature?

But, Hesper noted, there were no hunters in this tapestry. No men lying in wait behind the virgin's skirts. This was not that story.

No, whatever transpired between this Unicorn and the Lady was theirs alone, not the impetus of any man or predatory tradition. She, she herself, had captured him. The Unicorn had come willingly to lay his body across the thighs she spread for him. And though she held up the mirror and urged him to look at himself, at what he had become in her garden, he wanted only to look at her. And that made the Lady sad, somehow.

Hesper wondered what the Lady had wanted the Unicorn to see. Maybe she wanted him to see how strong and beautiful and free he could be, if only he would leave her behind. Maybe she feared what he would see in her and hoped to distract him from perceiving her for what she truly was. Someone who defined her own worth and her relationship with others by how tightly she could bind them to herself.

Projecting much? Hesper thought wryly. Behind her, Richard started whistling the same silly lullaby tune that had been stuck in her head earlier. She spun, laughing at the incongruity.

"Where'd you hear that?"

But the room was empty.

Unease rippled through her. It's an open floor plan, she told herself. Sound travels. Even all the windows were open to the cooling night air.

He could've been in the courtyard, and she'd have heard him. She padded softly through the house, an inexplicable dread keeping her footsteps light, her breaths quiet. "Richard?" she murmured, and immediately regretted it, the sound of her own voice chilling her.

A hush rolled through the air.

The walls of the house stared back at her, their gaze blank.

She walked outside, willing herself to look hard at every looming shadow and acknowledge they were only that: shadows. No lost little boy wandered here. No grief-stricken father. Surely if ghosts walked the earth, the Four Corners would be rife with them.

No sooner had she thought that, than she heard the dull, rhythmic pounding of a mortar and pestle, the soft murmur of voices rising beyond a crackling fire.

Woodpecker. Woodpecker, she told herself. Woodpecker and insects and night-birds and wind.

Pulling her robe close, she strode back indoors. Richard would come to bed when he was ready. Disappearing was a thing he did these days.

She closed the studio door before retreating to her own bedroom and closing that door, too. It was silly, but she didn't care for its gaping darkness. A barrier, however flimsy, pretended at refuge.

She thought of a little boy, barricaded. Goosebumps rose on her flesh.

She brushed her teeth, keeping her eyes on the sink, away from the space where a mirror should be. Was Leon Oberman staring down at her from the empty frame? Were his mournful eyes boring into the top of her head as she spit out the toothpaste and rinsed her mouth?

She nearly jumped out of her skin when the doorknob on the hallway facing door began to turn, stalling and rattling as it hit the lock she'd fastened out of habit.

"Hang on a second," she called to Richard. "I'm just getting ready for bed."

She unlocked the hallway door and exited through the bedroom door, closing it behind her so he could have some privacy. But when she slid under the sheets and propped her pillows for her nightly read, Richard was already there, his back rising and falling in heavy, regular breaths. Cold terror seized Hesper, and her eyes shot to the bathroom door she'd just shut, her ears straining. She could hardly hear over the pounding of her own heart.

But there was nothing to listen to. Not a whisper of movement. Not a hint of anything stirring anywhere in the house, and certainly not in the bathroom.

Calm down, she told herself. *Richard obviously was too*

tired to wait for you to finish up in the bathroom and came straight to bed. He'd always had a gift for falling asleep as soon as his head hit the pillow. What was the logical alternative? Someone broke into your house so they could use your bathroom?

One of the benefits of living so far out was that they'd be no target for crimes of opportunity. No random thieves or bored tweakers would trouble them here. And there was surely no reason for anyone to come out here on purpose. A schoolteacher and a moderately successful potter weren't exactly favorable marks for a heist. Anyone who came here hoping for hidden wealth would be sadly disappointed.

Hesper got up to switch on the window fan, grateful both for the dampening sound and the cool relief the breeze brought. It was remarkable how much the desert chilled at night. She eased back into bed, careful not to rouse her husband as she pulled up the covers.

Everything frightening you is in your head, she told herself firmly. The moon, the stars, the desert, even the house itself, embrace you in beauty. Let them. Let go of fear.

She opened her Agatha Christie novel and lost herself in the words. Hercule always made sense of the world. She didn't notice when the light under the bathroom door disappeared.

CHAPTER SEVEN

Only nine-thirty in the morning, and she was already a superhero.

That was what Hesper told herself, anyway. She'd measured the empty frame in the bathroom, called the glass company Gloria had recommended to order a replacement mirror, and even scheduled an appointment with the satellite internet company. She deserved some kind of gold star. She made do with a Hot Fudge Sundae Pop-Tart. With two of them, in fact.

Now that she'd disposed of the official adulting duties, the day was her own. And she had ideas.

She probably should have gotten an earlier start, but she'd had another rotten night. She hadn't had trouble sleeping, exactly. If anything, she'd felt positively drunk with exhaustion, her lids impossibly heavy every time she tried to drag them open. Broken dreams of a unicorn raging and weeping by turns and a lurking shadow-child broke again and again through the dark waters of unconsciousness. Hercule Poirot had been scolding her, but now she couldn't remember what he'd been so fussy about.

Oh, well. She figured soon enough she'd adjust to the desert's patterns. Rise early, nap during the heat of the afternoon. That was the ideal cycle, wasn't it? Then in the cool of the night, she and Richard could take a blanket outside and watch the stars fall.

And hope no scorpions or snakes decided to snuggle up with them. She grinned crookedly. Not a hazard she'd ever thought much about while trudging the sidewalks of Evanston, Illinois.

She'd intended to spend today at her wheel, but now she couldn't resist the allure of an explore. The house sat on twenty acres that were all her own. From her vantage point here, it looked as though this little copse of trees were all the forestation on the property, though plenty of juniper and scrub oak cropped up persistently here and there. No doubt these taller trees around the house had been painstakingly transplanted and watered by whoever had originally built the place. Who knew how much of her precious well water would be needed to keep them green? She hoped they were drought-tolerant species. Neglect-tolerant, too. Pampering plants was not a talent she possessed. Surely if they'd made it this long, they could survive her, too.

Hesper decided she loved the deceitfulness of the desert. From any angle, it looked uniform in color and topography, but start walking and all sorts of secrets revealed themselves: arroyos and ravines, canyons and cactus roses. The desert was a woman self-possessed. You had to love her before she gave up anything at all. You could not steal from her. You could only take what she offered, in her own time, in rations measured solely by her own hand.

And rations were what Hesper wanted today. She knew the aridity of this place was something of an illusion. One of the reasons she'd chosen this property was how the floods rained through the gorges here, and of course, the well had been a necessity. In Evanston, she'd always bought her clay. Here, she hoped to dig her own.

Getting the right recipe of clays to create durable pottery could be tricky, she knew, but she was eager to elevate her craft to a new level. A more intimate level. Digging for her own clay, purifying it, mixing it, would be a powerful alchemy. A connection with all the potters of the past, who had practiced the same craft for hundreds and thousands and tens of thousands of years before her.

She'd make mistakes, and it would take her some time to get the consistencies and the temperatures just right, but it would be worth it.

She loaded up her supplies. She had a high-sided wagon with fat tires she hoped would navigate the terrain well. Shiny and red, she'd bought it right before the move. Today would be its virgin voyage across the sands. A couple of buckets, some digging implements, a few bottles of water, a box of granola bars. She slathered herself with sunscreen and grabbed sunglasses and a floppy hat.

Scantily enough clad in a tank top and khaki shorts, she still wore thick socks and laced up her hiking boots over her ankles. She didn't intend to fall prey to blisters, sprained ankles, or snake bites.

Before she left the house, she made sure everything was turned off and all the windows open. An exquisite weightlessness suffused her limbs, something strangely close to joy bubbling under her skin. Locks were superfluous in this place. She didn't even have to close the front door if she didn't want to. Although she'd rather not come home to a coyote eating supper at her table, so close it she did. Still, until she'd arrived here, she hadn't truly realized how heavy the weight of everyone else's expectations and demands bore down on her. How living safely secured behind padlocks and bars and fences and gates had choked her of air she'd all but forgotten how to breathe.

In her new home, she could rise with cardinals and stay up all night talking to the stars if she wanted. She could let the sun turn her lights on for her, drink water from her own well, and listen to the birds sing and the wind chatter. She could dig her clay and create her pieces and walk in beauty, like the poem said. She could spend every day and night with her husband, where no voices or rumors or sad stories could reach them.

"You make me happy when skies are grey," she warbled as she walked, hauling the wagon behind her. Strength and energy poured through her. This was going to be a good day. Idly she wished Richard were there, but how silly would that be? That child of the north would melt away in heat like this.

Not to mention he wouldn't exactly experience the same spiritual connection with all the artists of the past she did while digging in the dirt. She giggled to herself at the notion of Richard crouched in a ravine, up to his elbows in clay and smeared with sweat.

No, it was just as well she'd left him to his books.

This late in the summer—it would already be early fall in Illinois, but she wasn't too sure of the season's cycle down here yet—only skeletons of the spring floods remained, gullies and arroyos and deep cracks that looked as if they hadn't known water for a thousand years. Lizards skittered across her path as she stepped quietly over the bare ground. Where life emerged, it burst from the earth without warning or fanfare, seemingly as likely to force its way through stone as the hard-packed dirt. Here junipers twisted, here sagebrush scented the air as sweetly and intoxicatingly as any English garden, here crisp-rattling grasses waved as stubbornly as if they feared neither heat nor drought. Hesper walked carefully to avoid stickers and cactus.

Something about the unpretentiousness of this place called to her. The desert did not apologize for what the ignorant called its inhospitality. She would not rob you of your survival, but neither would she gift it to you. She shared no sisterhood with the rich, wet forests of the north or lazy, sodden deltas of the south. She was not compelled to deck herself with flamboyant glories. She delighted in her thorns and thistles, the broad wrinkles crisscrossing her arid face, the tumbleweeds and scarred dead trees harboring hidden life. She didn't keep her affections for either the brash sun or the retiring moon to polite and respectable levels: she embraced them madly, unabashedly, burning and shivering by turns.

The desert was entirely herself, all the time. Hesper hoped she could learn to be the same.

By the time she'd filled her buckets and was heading back, though, she couldn't deny she was thinking longingly of the cool dimness beneath the roof of her little house. Her stiff fingers ached as she struggled to grip the wagon handle, reminding her of injury she'd prefer to forget. She swore she felt hot even on the inside of her skin. She'd drunk plenty of water, but still her head swam dizzily in the shimmering midday light. Through her broad-brimmed hat, the fingers of the sun pressed on her head like a hand of blazing iron. She trudged painfully back the way she'd come, imagining the wagon she dragged behind her was heavy as a train engine whose wheels had gone off the track.

Why had she gone so far? She'd definitely earned her cider today. Her malcontent was mostly bluster, though. Truly, she was delighted with the clay she found. And the difficulty in digging and retrieving it only added to its value. The pieces she crafted from this clay would hold her stumbling footsteps, her straining muscles, her muddied sweat. Her stupid hands and forgetful tendons. The alchemy of the pot lay in its power to transform the primal and physical labor of the potter into an object of beauty and purpose that fed the souls of people as ably as it fed their bellies.

She pictured children crouched around a campfire, their fingers scraping the bottom of their bowls as they scooped sticky rice into their mouths. Those hungry little fingers running over the same clay their grandmother's grandmothers had worked, that mother after mother had carefully wrapped away and gifted to her daughter as she made her own home. Pots were most magic when not on gallery shelves but on kitchen tables, Hesper was sure.

So when she made her pieces destined for gallery shelves, she did her best to evoke their true purpose. She didn't want to decorate cold rooms; she wanted to fill and warm bellies. Her pieces were intended as storytellers, squat grandmothers and grandfathers replete with stories. She hoped when people looked at her pots or hefted them in their hands, they saw old, familiar figures emerging from the mist of collective memory, hoped they felt the warmth and comfort of a cooking fire, heard the chanting murmur of ancient songs.

She managed to make it to the courtyard without passing out, which she considered a huge win. The desert did not play around, that was certain. She shouldn't have been so lackadaisical in her approach. Next time she would set an alarm, start right at dawn. She was exactly the sort of idiot who perished of heat exhaustion and left bones behind to feed the coyotes.

She left the wagon on the wide flagstones by the water spigot and went inside. She turned on the fans she'd set by the windows and splashed her face and shoulders from the kitchen faucet before sinking down onto the cool hardwood floors with a sigh. Chasing down the romance of clay in the wild was all well and good, but licorice sticks. She was glad to be back for now.

She loaded a couple of the cheap grocery-store croissants she'd bought with butter and cherry preserves and downed them with a lovely cold cider. Within a few minutes, she was feeling significantly restored. She peeked down the hallway before heading back outside. The studio door was still closed. No doubt Richard was in there, working on his lessons or reading. She wouldn't disturb him.

The next step in harvesting the clay she'd never done herself, only read about. She could always try the dry method—she certainly had sun enough for that—but she had the idea the wet method was preferred. It seemed like she could achieve a higher level of purity that way. So she filled the buckets partway with water from the hose, scooping and stirring the clumps of clay into a lovely slurry with her arms.

It's downright therapeutic, she thought. She could have lost herself in the rhythmic motion, in the slide and caress of thick, sloppy clay over her arms. She wasn't using or harvesting the clay, like some sort of conquistador or colonizer. She was working *with* the earth, laboring alongside to bring forth its beauty. In purifying and pulling out the clay, she became a midwife of possibilities. A gatekeeper of intentions.

Grunting and staggering, she managed to strain the stuff and bind it up in a cradle of well-washed sheets she'd bought for just this purpose. She loaded the bundles back in the wagon and trundled out to the trees that surrounded her home. She retrieved an eight-step ladder and set it up under a strong, broad limb.

Tying up the heavy sheets full of wet clay was significantly harder than she'd anticipated. She resolved to stop by the hardware store on her next trip to town. A heavy-duty hook or two knotted to the tree limb would make this task a thousand times easier. Then she could just tie a loop in the sheets and heft them up onto the hook. As usual, she was learning everything the hard way. If she'd paid more attention when reading about this, she'd have probably figured that out ahead of time. Or maybe if she'd taken physics seriously in high school. Pulleys and levers were a whole topic in that class, she seemed to remember.

Maybe. Maybe not. She was more of a hands-on learner,

for good or ill. Richard was the theoretical thinker in their household.

For no particular reason, her gaze wandered to the outhouse standing humbly deeper in the shade of the trees. Since the pump had been running thanks to her new solar power, she'd been more than happy to pretend it didn't even exist. Some remnant of dread clung to its wooden walls. As outhouses went, she supposed it was a rather nice one, but looking at it made fear swell in her throat.

The shadow-boy she'd seen had to have been nothing more than a figment of her imagination and a trick of the moonlight. Irritated by her own fancy, she strode over the pine needles and broken limbs and flung open the door.

Empty, of course. It was stuffy and hotter inside than out, which probably explained the few derelict spiderwebs. No doubt even the spiders preferred the cooler shade out under the trees. The little building was bigger than most of its kind: on a shelf sat a battered atlas, of all things, and a kerosene lantern was hanging from a hook. Hesper squinted at it, as if she could tell from looking if it worked.

Maybe Leon Oberman had sat out here daydreaming about road trips. The lid to the seat was down, and there was little odor to hint at its purpose. Like her, Leon had probably only used the place in a pinch. A breeze blew easily through the four Zia sun images cut high in the walls of the outhouse. A fitting departure from the moon silhouette she'd seen depicted on other outhouses. If anything, the outhouse smelled of pine and sage.

The door slammed shut behind her.

The wind, obviously, but still she yelped and jumped. There was no knob on the door, it just pushed open from the inside. The outside sported an iron handle for pulling. There wasn't even an interior lock or latch, as if no-one who'd lived here before had any reason to anticipate interruption.

She pushed.

Nothing happened.

Panic, mad and unreasoning, was immediate. She hurled herself against the broad door as well as she could, given the confines of the outhouse. "Let me out!" she screamed, though not a sound, not a breath, from the other side of the door suggested anyone around. "Let me out! Richard! Richard! Help me!"

She pounded and beat on the wood. She braced her feet against the bench seat and pushed with her back as hard as she could. Even the light wind which had been gusting had fallen into complete silence. She had a horrifying vision of being trapped here for days. Already her hair was matted to her head with sweat. No-one would check on her. No-one would come looking. Ginny would call, but she'd no doubt leave Hesper to her privacy for at least a while if she didn't answer.

Ginny! Hesper's fingers scrabbled in her pockets, but

she'd left her phone in the house hours ago.

She was going to die of heat stroke in an outhouse in the middle of the desert, completely alone. How horrifyingly ignominious.

She scrambled atop the bench seat, pressing her face against the cut-out sun-shapes, her eyes rolling in all directions. All she saw were stretching tree limbs and swaths of blue sky.

Behind her, the door swung open, its lazy creak sounding like a laugh.

Hesper all but fell off the bench in her frantic rush to get outside. She slammed the door shut behind her and leaned against it, gasping for air. Her head sawed back and forth, looking for any sign of what had slammed the door shut. Had held it shut. Had opened it after listening delightedly to her long minutes of terrorized alarm, crashing against the walls.

The woods were empty. Forcing herself to slow down, to think rationally, she pulled the door open again, examining its edges. It must have simply gotten stuck somehow. Must have. Wedged closed. Maybe the door wasn't square. Maybe there was some sap or goo that had briefly glued the door shut in the heat. But the wood felt smooth under her fingers, opening and closing repeatedly with no effort.

Hesper backed away from the outhouse. She didn't care if the solar panels failed or the well pump went out. If she couldn't use the toilet in the house, she was going to squat behind a tree somewhere. No way in ham sandwiches was she risking getting trapped in there again. She pushed her damp hair off her forehead.

As she bent to pick up the wagon handle, she glanced toward the house. There, gazing out from the living room window, a dark figure with shining eyes of light watched her.

Adrenaline pushed the fear out of her body. Adrenaline and fury.

"Hey!" she yelled, taking off for the house at a run. Rather than disappearing, the figure raised a hand in a taunting wave. She tore around the front of the house, through the courtyard, and in the front door.

"You are my sunshine, my only sunshine," she heard a childish voice trilling, as if from far away and getting farther. The living room stood empty, like the kitchen.

She thudded down the hallway, flinging open the doors to her bedroom, the bathroom, the studio. Even the linen closet. No sign of the shadow-boy remained.

Richard stood abruptly as she thundered into the studio. "What's the matter?"

"A boy," she rattled. "The boy. He was here. In the house. He locked me in the outhouse. Didn't you hear me yelling for help? Why didn't you hear me?"

Richard set his hands gently, almost gingerly, on her shoulders. She hated the careful expression on his face. She missed their old recklessness with one another. He handled her so gently these days.

"There's no one here," he said softly. "No one at all. Only you."

His words seemed to echo. She went cold. Why did he say things like that?

"No," she insisted. "I saw him. He was in the window. He locked me in the outhouse."

"How could he have locked you in the outhouse if he was in the house? Have you had anything to drink lately? You're soaked through with sweat. And look—you've tracked mud all through the house. Come on. There's no boy."

He took her hand and led the way back through the home, room by room. She followed meekly, equally abandoned by certainty and terror. She felt only empty now.

"There. See? No boy. Not in the house, not in the courtyard, not in the yard." Richard even opened the outhouse door and poked his head in. "No one here. The door just stuck on you. I don't know why you were in there, anyway. The bathroom in the house is working fine."

"You're right," she said meekly, her head drooping. "I don't know what happened."

"Drink some water instead of that cider and eat a little protein. You're pushing yourself too hard. Have you been taking your meds?"

She glared.

"Okay, okay."

Hesper let her head fall onto her arms on the kitchen table. Richard was right. She was tired and hot and apparently flighty. What was the alternative? That a ghost-boy who had never even lived here had locked her in an outhouse for all of five minutes and then run off?

"I'm my own worst enemy," she said.

CHAPTER EIGHT

Hesper was accustomed to Richard's nocturnal wanderings, but it was always disconcerting to reach across the sheets and find him gone. Every time, her brain almost went too far, every time her heart lurched over before she could catch her breath and mutter hastily, "It's okay, it's okay, it's okay."

As mantras went, hers wasn't the most sophisticated, but it worked. It threw up the roadblock she needed. She'd been much further down that bleak concrete nightmare in the past, with its shattered buildings and black staring windows. She refused to accept what waited there. So when she bumped into the sawhorse barriers with their warning signs, she heeded them hastily and turned back around.

Hesper lay still and quiet, only the sheet covering her bare body. The fan hummed softly. Outside the open window, insects squeaked and chirped and whistled. There was a sparseness to the music of the night here. Rather than a general chorus, far away neighbors called greetings across great distances. The limbs of the trees surrounding the house creaked softly as a gentle wind pushed them into each other's arms. Hesper pictured them like a semi-circle ring of sweet-faced crones, their tangled arms raised to the stars as they swayed around the house they stood to protect.

Hesper thought of her new tapestries on the wall in the living room. *Hearing* was the second in the series, and probably her least favorite. It looked so sedate and joyless, unmistakably so in her opinion when contrasted with the emotions music was supposed to elicit in the human heart. On a whim, she slid out of bed. Wrapping her robe around her, she stole soundlessly down the hall to the living room.

She switched on a table lamp, content with its faint illumination. She stood close to the wool panels, her eyes unstitching the shadows from the threads as she struggled to decipher the tapestry's import.

The Lion and the Unicorn both looked happy enough. And what in the world had the Unicorn been eating lately? No longer the sleek, swift, and savage creature of the forest deep, he looked more like a rather wobbly fat lapdog. Perhaps too much civilization had done him in. Happens to the best of us, she thought cheerlessly.

All of the other little animals looked equally delighted, leaping playfully across the field of flowers as birds flew overhead and the pennants waved gaily. But it was the expressions of the Lady and the lady-in-waiting who drew Hesper's attention. Though they were the ones producing the music on the funny little instrument that Hesper didn't recognize, the music that created such an atmosphere of stultified contentment among the garden's other residents, the faces of the two women were drawn and somber.

Did they know their role was only to distract and occupy? Did they take no pleasure in the music because it was the theme of their own captivity? Did the Lady regret the domesticity that had robbed the Lion of his fierceness and reduced the Unicorn to a portly pet? What sort of lies did the music tell to persuade them all to stay safely inside their little floating island of flowers? Lies that the Lady and her maid found unconvincing but dully continued to play, play, play, as if their role in the tableau could afford no rebellion.

What was the cost of such collaboration? Compelled or no, seducing other souls to their own thrall had to take a heavy toll. Something stirred in Hesper's mind, something uncomfortable and restless. Something heavy with untruths that rattled like chains.

Soberly Hesper clicked off the lamp. She drifted unhurriedly back up the dark hallway, lost in thought. She wasn't sure whether people's tendency to lie to themselves was one of humanity's best survival hacks or their most dangerous inclination. Maybe it was both. Surely there were moments in life a person could never walk through if they were forced to confront them in all their stark and awful reality.

But getting stuck in the illusion, like the Lady and her lady-in-waiting, must be equally perilous. As blissful as that Unicorn looked, he couldn't know how slow and fat he'd become. The Lion didn't realize his teeth were blunted. If happiness required a person to deny the fundamental truths of their own nature, could it be happiness at all? Or were the lies as dangerous a drug as any heroin? She rolled her shoulders, anxiety running like ants under her skin.

She went to the bathroom before returning to bed, not bothering to switch on the light as she went. She knew where her own ass was, after all. But as she washed her hands, her perception tilted crazily when she automatically raised her gaze to the darkness where the empty mirror frame stood.

A whole world opened up between the wooden arms of the frame. Hesper clutched the edges of the sink, as if she might get pulled through, but she felt no tugging sensation. Instead, images rolled and curved away from her like movie scenes playing on either side of some long hallway. No fear intruded this time. Longing propelled her instead, an intense desire to understand. To see. Almost, to remember. As if there were something or someone she'd dearly loved but had managed to forget, someone she could only find again here, in this moment.

On one side, Hesper saw the man she recognized easily as Leon Oberman. A sort of happiness, almost gaiety, infused the action. He could have been in any big city. New York or Houston or Los Angeles or Denver. Busy sidewalks and glass-front shops. He walked with purpose, meeting with shiny people in shiny clothes with shiny smiles. Hesper caught glimpses of his paintings hanging on walls in multiple galleries. He was feted, hugged, clapped on the back, as if artists constituted some sort of lucky Buddha belly for rich people.

One person was different, though. A woman with striking eyes and flyaway hair. Again and again she appeared. She seemed to disappear every time Leon reached her, till the last panel, which ran on a glitchy loop that Hesper's eyes struggled to follow. Leon didn't appear here, and Hesper realized she was looking through his gaze across a cracked café table. The woman's hands grasped his, a sensation somehow both exciting and comforting. She was laughing and talking, her mobile face lit with an otherworldly light. Hesper was transfixed, transported. The music of the woman's voice, indecipherable yet irresistible, flowed over her.

Another feeling intruded then, dark and menacing and desperate. Something was tugging at her consciousness, pleading and frantic. Reluctantly she tore her attention away from the café and found herself drawn along the other side of the moving-picture hallway. The side she knew, somehow, Leon couldn't see. Not while he sat, unburdened and hopeful, at that café table.

Happiness permeated here, too, but it was underlaid with resignation. Or maybe dread. Images of Leon's son, in Leon's arms, at his knee, bouncing down the street alongside him. Floppy hair and fat little fingers and a sunny smile. Leg braces and a bicycle helmet and sneakers with Velcro instead of laces. Throwing pennies in city fountains and playing together in children's museum sandboxes. Aquariums and planetariums and preschool classrooms and strangers with too-kind smiles. His son on his hip at gallery openings or playing on the floor during interviews. Trust shining in his eyes.

Then the last scene, on the same jerking loop as the café scene. The child shivering in a rain jacket, his umbrella flipped inside out by the wind. Hair plastered to his wide forehead. His expression, miserable and expectant. Waiting for his father. A father, for once, for only once, forgetful.

Hesper's gaze swung back to the café, noting for the first time the droplets sliding down the windows. The reels shuddered to a stop, dissipating into fog till only the inky darkness of the bathroom remained. Hesper dragged in a shaking breath.

She stumbled back to bed, dropping her robe with a whoosh before she slipped back under the covers. Suddenly the room felt icy cold. She wished Richard had come back to bed. His cold calves wouldn't offer much comfort to her chilly toes, but she'd sure like the company. She had no doubt what she'd just seen.

That must be Leon's story of his son's death. She wished she knew the boy's name. Tomorrow she would do some digging. Surely it would be relatively easy to find on the Internet. And it suddenly felt important that she call the child by his name. He wasn't a blank gravestone somewhere or a malevolent shadow-boy conjured by her wild imagination. He'd just been a little boy who loved his dad, who'd died too young, weakened by the same trick of fate that had dictated the circumstances of his birth.

Clearly Leon blamed himself for what had happened. And maybe some of it even was his fault. From what she could decipher, Leon must have forgotten to pick his son up or been late because he'd been so caught up with his café date. A thoroughly human error, but an error nonetheless.

"But your devotion was at least equally evident," Hesper whispered, as if Leon could hear her.

Not just devotion, either. More than obligation, Leon had delighted in his son. He hadn't resented the duties of single fatherhood. He'd loved his son. Enjoyed him. Wanted him. Wanted him more than anything. The thoughtlessness that Leon blamed for his son's death hadn't been indicative of a general neglect. It had been the heedlessness of an instant, a single mistake islanded by years of care and attentiveness.

An accident. Just a terrible, terrible accident.

The words sounded loud as a crash in the dark bedroom, loud as a massive tree limb cracking and falling heavily through glass and steel. Loud as a man's neck breaking in a passenger seat. Hesper keened and yanked the covers over her head, curling into the fetal position and closing her eyes as tightly as she could. *Sleep*, she needed to sleep.

"It's okay, it's okay, it's okay," she bit out between clenched teeth.

CHAPTER NINE

"That sounds like some dream," Ginny said.

"I'm not so sure it was a dream," Hesper said, slapping together a turkey sandwich and directing her voice toward the phone on the counter. "I felt wide awake. And I'd just been in the living room, staring at your weird tapestries."

"Oh, so the tapestries are weird, but I'd like to point out that you're the one wandering around in the middle of the night meditating on them. You have all day to look at those things. I refuse to accept responsibility for this."

"I couldn't sleep. And I started thinking about them, so I figured I'd take a closer look. That's why you sent them, isn't it? To be some sort of bizarre witchy guides on my hero's journey?"

Ginny chuckled without rancor. "I'm that transparent, huh?"

"Subtle you are not."

"Life is too short to drop hints. Speaking of which, have you been taking your meds? Do you need help getting your prescriptions transferred to a pharmacy down there? I'd be happy to call for you."

Hesper's mind flashed to the prescription bottles lined up neatly on the edge of the bathroom sink when she'd gotten up this morning. She suspected Richard and his sister were conspiring against her. With the best possible intention, of course. But conspiring nonetheless.

She'd swept up the bottles and placed them neatly back inside the unmirrored cabinet.

"No worries," she said breezily. "It's just a phone call. Nothing I can't handle. I've even been to the store. Maybe I'll find a coffee shop and do some people watching."

"Oh, that's excellent. Maybe the change in scenery was exactly what you needed. A radical shift. And people-watching in Santa Fe has to be world-class, right? It's such a destination for all sorts."

"No doubt. Besides, at some point, I have to figure out where all the best food is—the best green chili, the best margarita. The best mole sauce. Santa Fe might be an art mecca, but it's a foodie mecca too. I don't want to squander my opportunity."

Ginny laughed again, and Hesper knew she'd hit the right note to quell her sister-in-law's anxiety. Or so she thought, till Ginny circled back. Like a bojangled coyote.

"But seriously, Hesper. You don't think this Leon Oberman is really trying to communicate with you, do you?"

She could outright lie to Ginny, she supposed, to make her feel better. But for all the grief it brought her, she'd never had that sort of relationship with her sister-in-law. For better or for worse, they leveled with each other.

"I don't know. Maybe it's all my imagination. Maybe my brain is taking the few pieces of information it's gathered and is trying to put them together into a cohesive story for me for some reason. But those scenes last night—they felt intimate. Specific. Real. Very, very real."

"What about the other things you've seen? That shadow-boy sounded really frightening. Dark and evil and not like an innocent little boy who died too young. What if you're conjuring these things up to punish yourself somehow?"

The roadblock again. Flashing lights and danger signs. Hesper veered back. Not going that way. No way, no how.

"Try not to worry, Ginny. You know I came out to the desert to learn. To listen. There have to be a thousand stories here, and it's gonna be great for my art. I'm just taking it all a little too much to heart, maybe. Anyway, I need to eat my sandwich before I perish, and how sad would you be then?"

"All right, I'll let you go. Just don't spend too much time obsessing on that man, okay? He's long gone, his suffering is over. You don't need to take his anguish on as your own. You deserve a beautiful life. I need you to believe that, okay?"

"Yes, dear. I'm good enough, I'm smart enough, and doggone it, people like me!"

"You're hopeless. But I love you! Call me later."

Hesper took a big bite of her sandwich and chewed, washing it down with a tall glass of cool water. Maybe she should take a bit of a break from Ginny. They'd been talking on the phone every other day for months now. Frankly, her life wasn't interesting enough to constitute that many conversations. Ginny would probably like a break herself. Hesper knew Ginny thought she was keeping Hesper tied to her sanity with the slenderest of threads. That had to be a burden.

Yeah. She'd just let the phone go to voicemail the next time Ginny called. Maybe the next two times. By the time they talked again, she'd have better stories. More to report. And Ginny could enjoy a little freedom from her half-crazy relation. Felka was sure to appreciate it, too. Hesper liked Felka, and they'd always got on, but lately, she'd caught Felka watching her with an expression of constant concern. Dismay, even.

Every family needed a break from time to time. This would be good. Healthy. A respite for all.

She'd gotten a late start today. Those midnight meanderings took a toll. Not that it mattered. She had no schedule to keep, after all. Sometime this afternoon the satellite guy would be here. Once he had her hooked up, she'd check in on her email. She could have done that already using her phone, but she was kind of enjoying feeling disconnected for a few days. The gallery managers where her work was displayed, though, always wanted continual connection, whenever the whim seized them. A little forced patience on their part wouldn't go amiss, she mused. All the experts swore less screen time was better for everyone, right?

But she'd adult properly later.

The sun was already high in the sky, heat reflecting off the ground. She cast a longing glance at the foot-powered wheel set up in the courtyard. It looked so peaceful. So sound. So grounded and connected to the past. Hesper supposed that was one of her favorite things about throwing clay. She was never alone when she sat at the wheel. She could hear the humming of thousands of other wheels spinning away as she worked, hear the songs and mutterings and tongue-clicks of all the other potters who had ever cast a pot.

But however romantic the old-fashioned clatter of the foot-powered wheel, the communion of other potters was no less present at the electric wheel. There was nothing inherently more valid about doing things the hard way just for the sake of the hard way. Any ancient potter would have been beyond delighted by an electric wheel, she had no doubt. And probably downright baffled by her nostalgic affection for the foot-powered variety.

Finishing up the last of her crust, Hesper walked across the living room to consider the third tapestry Ginny had sent her. *Touch.* Three pennants or sigils or coats-of-arms or whatever they were called, just like Ginny had said. Oh. And wasn't this one the anomaly? She looked at the last panel, *A Mon Seul Desir.*

Yep. Three on that one too. So it was out of order? Or

maybe it was much simpler than that. Maybe this was the mystery unfolded right here. Everyone wondered exactly what the Lady's one desire was, right? Maybe the tapestries themselves answered that question.

Maybe the last panel had the same number of pennants as the third because the third panel was the response to the question the last panel asked. What the Lady desired most, what she desired only, was whatever was revealed in the third panel. In *Touch*.

And how very apt a conclusion was that for a potter to draw. People tended to think of pottery as a visual art, but Hesper found that incidental. Pottery was the consequence of the most sensual, the most carnal of all the disciplines. The product took its power from all the straining muscles and bent bones and sweating flesh of the artist. A potter expended her entire body and soul drawing forth the simplest being from the clay. Like the Divine Themselves.

It wasn't just the Genesis account that told of God fashioning their people from clay. All around the world, people recounted tales of a Creator whose favorite object was born of the dirt, breathed into life by an exhalation of the divine soul. Maybe there were a few steps missing from a scientific point of view, but as myths went, Hesper didn't suppose anything could be more true.

And so she too pursued the call of the divine. Looking into the dirt and finding the beautiful. Eschewing the despair of mud and choosing the possible.

Obviously she was biased, but nonetheless she found Touch easily the most compelling of the six panels.

The lady-in-waiting was nowhere to be seen. This was the only panel where the Lady's gaze extended beyond the garden. She was looking out, far beyond the confines of her little island, beyond even the sea of flowers that bounded her haven. She stood tall and strong, her hair untethered, her hand firmly grasping the Unicorn's horn as if to lead him to whatever distant land her gaze was set on. She was irresistible. Inexorable.

The raw sexuality and power of that pose was impossible to miss. Hesper wondered at the man who had created it, at the weavers who'd brought it to life, at the family who'd hung it in their halls. At the women, bound in corsets and chaperones and expectations, who had walked beneath this Lady. How they must have envied her. Had they ever believed in her? Ever thought a woman walking fearlessly toward the unknown, with her desires firmly grasped in her hand, could exist? Or had she only been a myth, a fairytale whose magic they could never hope to claim for themselves? Had they kept their gaze downcast, safe from temptation, or had they lingered, longing to share her epicurean pursuits?

Contrary to what Hesper suspected the Church and the courts of the day would have had to say, nature itself seemed to approve of the Lady's choice. The Lion, who might have represented the martial defenses of society and virtue, smiled happily to see his erstwhile rival chosen to join the Lady in her rebellion against those orders. The Unicorn himself was fearless. His eyes rested serene and unquestioning on the Lady who directed him—he trusted her, unreservedly, to lead the way.

A small detail, but so very intriguing: almost all the other little animals who had bounded merrily across the panels looked unhappy in this tapestry, collared and chained. Only the birds flew free and the rabbits leapt untethered. Hesper didn't find that incongruous at all. Those creatures had been perfectly content to find their happiness in this beautiful prison, so why should the realities of their enslavement be hidden any longer? The birds, by contrast, had always known what lay beyond this diminutive world. And rabbits always represented sexual proclivities and desires, so how could they possibly be tamed or leashed?

However lovely or luxurious, the garden was still a cell, in the end. But perhaps the birds had whispered to the lady of what lay beyond. Certainly she had to have longed after the freedom that was so effortlessly theirs. As for the rabbits—well, even in medieval times, rabbits mirrored boundless sexuality, if sometimes cloaked in the only slightly more circumspect specter of its inevitable consequences.

Hesper thought it notable that the lady-in-waiting was

missing here as well. In choosing the Unicorn and all he represented—sensuality, power, liberty, savagery—the Lady was renouncing her former life and its trappings. In her new life, she would have no need of a lady-in-waiting to meet her needs. She and the Unicorn would serve one another and be content, perfectly complete in one another. In this panel, the Lady even held the pennant herself. She was her own standard-bearer. What clearer proclamation of freedom could there be? Not only did the Lady and the Unicorn tapestries eschew any images whatsoever of men or their influence, the artist had assigned to the Lady all the powers that men in his society had claimed for themselves alone.

Downright revolutionary, Hesper reflected.

She shook her head. She hadn't researched any of this herself, of course, but based on what Ginny had told her, she thought the scholars (as usual) made this much harder than they needed to. Sure, maybe a treatise on feminine power and liberation was highly unusual for its day, but these pieces hadn't survived for hundreds of years because they were mediocre, had they? In her opinion, modern people were always quick to assume that their feelings and conflicts and perspectives were new, all the product of their privileged and enlightened education. But Hesper didn't think so.

She stroked the silken threads of the Unicorn's flank and cast a hard smile on the Lady. "You keep your eyes on the outside, Lady," she murmured. "You're gonna make it."

Richard was nowhere to be seen when Hesper entered her studio. Just as well, otherwise she'd have had to chase him out. They didn't really have a choice but to share a workspace. They'd never had the sort of resources to justify a separate library and studio. At least this room was much bigger than their cramped apartment rooms in Evanston. And having the courtyard to work in was a luxury almost too expansive to grasp.

The window over Richard's desk stood open. Hesper had dragged a pedestal fan in here a day or so ago and set it up by the desk. It was remarkable how comfortable the house felt with all the windows open and the fan blowing shaded air through the open floorplan. No doubt it helped that she hardly used any electricity besides the refrigerator and the fans themselves. But those ancient architects really knew what they were doing with these massive stucco walls. The heat gathered during the day was released comfortably in the chilly night hours, and then by morning, the house felt fresh and cool. No doubt it helped she hadn't used the oven yet, either.

The next couple of hours passed in a fugue more powerful than any drug could produce. The song of wheel, the resistance of the clay, the slippy, sweet seduction of water and earth and maybe. Maybe, Hesper was sure, was the most powerful ingredient in any artistic endeavor. There was the will of the medium being manipulated, the will of the artist doing the manipulating, and then there was the maybe. The unseen, undreamt reality that emerged in resistance and in concord with both forces.

She hummed as she bent, straining, to her task. Thighs squeezing, fingers pushing, pulling. Sweat pooling in the small of her back. Her squat little tree, emerging from the earth and its wild rotations.

"You are my sunshine, my only sunshine..."

Serenity spread through her chest as she fashioned the pot. This was the last of a series she was completing for the Hollow Night Gallery. The pots were squat, satisfyingly earthy and unapologetic for the space they occupied. Thick roots spread from their bases, and their handles branched upward. Together, the four pots would represent the World Tree and the cardinal directions. The other three pots were packed safely away on her newly assembled shelves, fully finished, and Hesper knew Marcy DeLilio, the gallery manager, was anxiously waiting for the complete collection.

For her part, Hesper was excited to try her kiln for the first time in its new home. But there was no hurrying this step of the process. Pottery demanded patience above all. Anticipation led to ruin. So she set the pot aside to begin its drying process. It would be weeks before she could pack and mail the entire collection, which would be its own exercise in patience and care. Marcy would have to keep waiting. But she'd known about the move. Her protestations would be perfunctory.

Hesper was washing when she heard the satellite installer pull up. She endured the usual patronizing rigmarole as the installer attempted to convince her of the great difficulty of his task, commensurate only with his great ability. She smiled and nodded only as long as she absolutely had to, then left him to it. Why did men always need to be told what a good job they were doing, how strong and capable they were? She sighed. Happily she had to accommodate little enough of that anymore.

Sure enough, he managed to accomplish his herculean task in a reasonable amount of time. Clearly under the impression he was dealing with an unattached woman, he made a valiant effort to engage her in a conversation about the solar system in a failed bid at flirtation, but she didn't play along. And she wasn't fooled, anyway: his interest was more habit, a knee-jerk reaction to finding himself alone with a single woman, than any sincere attraction. Her hands were clean enough, but she was still covered in clay water, her face unpainted, her hair wild.

It was a relief to send him back on his way and have her little enclave restored to solitude. She enjoyed another delightfully long shower before settling into her recliner with her laptop to catch up on all the communications she'd been willfully missing the last few days. A couple of tomato-jalapeno-and-grilled-cheese sandwiches sufficed for an easy supper. And when she was done being a grown-up, maybe she could stream a few true-crime documentaries with her new luxurious bandwidth. Might as well treat herself. She giggled.

Holy ham sandwiches. There were a lot of emails. Most of them were spam, of course, but still. Why did people require so much attention?

She had messages from her parents and from Richard's. Ginny was the only one who had the nerve to just call anymore. Hesper took her time writing those replies, doing her best to make the new place sound idyllic and throwing in a few photos for good measure. Her family wanted reassurance, she knew. She hadn't had the emotional resilience to bear up under the weight of their needs for a long time, but it wasn't that she didn't understand or didn't care. She didn't have anything to offer, that was all. So she tried hard to infuse what little communication she could manage with hope.

Sure enough, there was a polite check-in from Marcy at Hollow Night. Hesper rattled off that reply with little effort. A couple of pieces at other galleries had sold, which would mean a welcome infusion in her bank account when she checked it. And a new gallery, whom Marcy had recommended, wanted her to send along a portfolio for review.

All in all, it was dark by the time she'd caught up. She

padded back into the kitchen for a glass of cider topped off with a generous shot of Fireball. She started dozing long before detectives had even found the third body, so she snapped her laptop shut and retreated to her bedroom. Bleary faced, she couldn't resist peering into the empty mirror frame as she brushed her teeth, but only bare wood stared back. She figured even her imagination was too sleepy to play games with her tonight.

She'd have felt differently if she'd seen the dark figure of a hollow-eyed man sitting on the foot of her bed as she slept, mournfully singing *You Are My Sunshine* in a low, broken voice.

CHAPTER TEN

She could do this, Hesper told herself stoutly the next morning. The whole reason for this move was so she could become part of a new and vibrant community of artists. New to her, that is. One of the oldest anywhere, by the measure of world history. She couldn't accomplish that by burying herself out here with the arroyos and the cactus. She needed more than lizards and dragonflies to learn from.

Before the accident, she'd never felt more at home than when wandering city streets studded with galleries, studios, cafes, and gift shops. The energy rising from the sidewalks, a sort of collective harmony of the seekers of beauty and its crafters, fed her veins. She'd known all the shop owners and gallery managers and museum curators and baristas from one end of the state to the other. But like a wounded animal, she'd retreated entirely when she'd finally been released from the hospital after the accident. And the reluctance to rejoin a world that no longer held the sheen of reality to her had become a dread more powerful than she'd have ever predicted.

But look how well she'd done at the grocery store, Hesper told herself with false cheer. Besides, what choice did she have? Any chance she stood at survival relied entirely on her ability to make a place for herself in this society. And it wasn't as if there was any shortage of artists in New Mexico.

Some of the world's foremost creatives in every imaginable discipline made the Four Corners their home. Carving out a niche for herself here would require humility and dedication.

Cowering would get her nowhere.

Still, when she opened the kitchen cabinet to get a drinking glass, she couldn't help looking envyingly at the little boy who gazed out at her from the wooden surface. Although the subject was always the same, each painting was distinct, unique in its representation and the feelings it evoked. In this one, the child's eyes were pensive, drifting. As if he saw a future no-one else perceived.

Son of a cinnamon stick. She still needed to find out his name. Tonight, when she got home, she promised herself. Research.

As she closed the cabinet door, she wished desperately she could climb into the darkness beside the boy and let the cool, quiet, dark insulate her from the rest of the world, as it did him. But she didn't deserve that sort of peace, did she?

She scarfed down some peanut butter toast and forced herself out to the car. She waved disconsolately to the house in the rearview mirror. "Be back soon."

Today, she was avoiding the square proper. Besides the Indian Market, where native crafters and artisans lined the sidewalk under the awnings with all sorts of jewelry and art objects inspired by ancient patterns and methods, most of the shops in the square were solidly targeted at tourists.

Although all of Santa Fe might be described as a tourist town, some of the galleries and shops had customers who were looking for something more than a dreamcatcher and a pretty silver knife. That was where Hesper was headed. Somewhere that featured something besides pretty trinkets but also where her identity as a completely non-Native potter wouldn't be a terminally crippling handicap. Perhaps in time, she would be able to learn from the local tribal communities, but she would never be in competition with them. Only informed and bettered by them, she hoped.

Rambling away in her head, she was only distracting herself from the task at hand. She'd been parked outside this gallery she'd found online for ten minutes already. Only late morning, but it was already way too hot to be sitting in a car. She had to get out of here and in those glass doors before her mascara melted.

She was not mistaken in how much better the cold air conditioning felt when she stepped inside. She had definitely been spoiled by the years of central air in her Illinois apartment.

A young man with bored eyes stepped forward to greet her. "Have you visited us before?"

"No, I actually just moved to town. I'm a potter myself, so I'm just out getting a sense of the various galleries in town. Would it be possible to schedule a meeting with the gallery manager?"

If possible, he looked even more self-consciously bored as she spoke. Hesper didn't doubt that places like this were inundated year-round with hopeful artists at all levels of craft and all stages of their professional career, but she suspected his disdain had at least as much to do with the fact that she referred to herself as a potter rather than a ceramic artist.

She understood the current adoption of the more fanciful title. An assertion of the craft as a valued art in its own right, a distinction from the human production lines who used molds to mass-produce whatever bit of nonsense a tourist or a semi-woke soccer mom might buy. But Hesper cherished her connection to the humblest intent of the work. The great work. The original work. Pots held food for the hungry and stories for the soul. Ashes of the dead, promises for the unborn. A small thing, that she rarely justified or explained, but in her own way, refusing to be called anything but a potter was her way of honoring all the grandmothers and grandfathers who threw clay before her.

At any rate, she wasn't inclined to feel defensive in front of someone whose job consisted of greeter and cashier. Did that make her a bitch? Maybe. She was okay with that.

The man sniffed. "Our gallery is typically booked up many months in advance, and the rotation is highly competitive. Our artists are world-class—"

"That information is all available on your website,"

Hesper interrupted. "I'm not in need of an explanation of how galleries operate. I asked if I could make an appointment. If you lack access to your manager's calendar, perhaps you can direct me to someone who can help me."

She watched a dark flush rise from under his collar before he turned stiffly away and marched back to his counter. He reached underneath and retrieved a battered paper calendar. Hesper figured gallery owners would still be using the same old paper calendars when the robot overlords took over. When it worked, it worked.

"The soonest Mr. Iglesias could meet with you is two weeks out."

"No problem. I'm here to stay." Hesper pulled out her phone. She, unlike the gallery owners she knew, intended to beat the robot overlords at their own game when the time came. "How about Wednesday the twenty-fouth?"

She kept her eyes on her phone so that she wouldn't grin, knowing how irritated he had to be as she took the power in the conversation back out of his hands.

"Umm...yes, that should work. Two in the afternoon?"

"Perfect. I'll leave you my card, in case Mr. Iglesias wants to check out my website prior to our meeting. Thank you for your assistance. I'm going to take a look around now."

"Certainly."

He had a gift for making what should have been a welcoming acquiescence sound exactly like getting kicked out. She couldn't resist smiling broadly in his direction at that.

Hesper loved galleries. Loved everything about them. How the best were practices in absence, in void, in emptiness, allowing each artist featured to spill a piece of themselves into the space so that the artist alone was perceived as existing. She'd been in storefronts that were all ambience and mood lighting and wax burners, but as far as she was concerned, those were hobby projects for rich people with too much time on their hands and no taste, not serious businesses.

This one, despite the snooty kid in the shiny suit, was no overwrought weekend project. She saw a couple names she recognized and many she didn't. Something deep inside her thrummed softly at the prospect of all the new artists she had to meet here, the new rhythms and patterns of thought and creative impulses she would learn. Art communities were like tributaries, distinct in their topography, but all flowing into the same Great River. The idea of bivouacking her little canoe to a new shore and slipping off into the stream thrilled her.

It would almost be like being alive again.

Almost.

Her mind shuddered away from the thought. She'd been doing everything she could to bury herself for months now. Fresh air and rushing currents weren't for her. Ash and earth, those were her inheritances. Just the thought of exhilaration, of something like joy, filled her with horror and shame.

Go through the motions, that was all she needed to do. Make the rounds, do the work. Whatever would allow her to continue her art. Because the art was all she had left. No matter how long or how hard she worked to better her craft, there would always be an aspect of the process that originated outside of her. A muse, the collective consciousness, the tendency of the universe itself toward beauty. However you wanted to think of it. And she owed herself to recognize that. To honor that obligation, however tenuous a thread that might seem to others, was all the *raison d'etre* she had left.

It would have to do. Already she regretted the little boost of energy she'd gotten from her repartee with the young man who now was doing his best to look important and busy. Now she just felt dirty and small. Who was she to rob him of his pitiful armor, anyway?

The door tinkled as she left. She consulted her list. Two more within walking distance, then she'd need to get back in the car.

Regardless of all she'd accomplished back in Chicago, it was impossible not to feel daunted and overwhelmed by the galleries here. It certainly wasn't as if Chicago lacked for an energy and force of its own. But there was something about

Santa Fe. Something at once primal and sophisticated, fundamental and daring. Magic breathed in this place, inescapable and undeniable.

She'd visited eight galleries by the time she spotted it. At a glance, it might be mistaken for a canvas in motion, all color and light, but almost immediately the eyes were drawn to focus on an image emerging effortlessly through the wild, passionate hues: a raven on the wall of an old Spanish mission. Although the subject couldn't have been more different, she immediately recognized the hand.

Leon Oberman.

Sure enough, when she hurried across the Berber carpet to read the name on the little bronze plaque underneath the painting—which was massive, the canvas alone standing at least four feet tall, her fingers traced the now-familiar name printed there.

Matilde, the gallery owner she'd been chatting with a few moments earlier, noted her interest and came to join her.

"It's a phenomenal piece, isn't it? I actually purchased it outright to be part of my permanent collection when the artist died."

"It's stunning."

"Leon had a rare gift for evoking unexpected emotion with his paintings. People try to explain it—his use of color, the style of his brush strokes, the way he frames and reframes reality itself—but I don't like to examine it too much. I just let it do its work."

"Did you know him personally?"

"Oh, yes. We sold quite a few of his pieces. We were only acquainted for a few months, though. He passed away not long after he moved here."

Hesper's respect for the tidy little older woman grew exponentially as she realized Matilde had no intention of using Leon's sensational death as a selling point.

"I bought his house," Hesper heard herself volunteer.

The other woman started.

"Really? I knew it had been on the market for some time." Matilde glanced over, her dark eyes narrowed in sudden suspicion. Her lips tightened, and she drew herself up stiffly. Hesper could see it written all over: the gallery owner thought she was some kind of ghoul-hunter. Hesper hurried to explain.

"I'm afraid I didn't know anything about him before I made the offer. I bought the place sight unseen from Chicago. I'd been dreaming about becoming part of the artist community here since my husband and I came out on a honeymoon trip years ago. The realtor was required to tell me someone died in the house, of course, but I didn't know he was an artist until I moved in. At the time, I was just grateful the price was low enough for me to afford."

Hesper's confidence softened Matilde a little. "You'd never heard of him?"

Hesper shook her head. "I didn't even think to ask the name of the previous owner until I found his paintings in the house. I bought the property from the bank, you know, not from his estate or anything."

Matilde's eyes sparked. "Paintings? They sold paintings along with the house?"

"Not on purpose. In fact, they tried to hide them."

"Tried to hide a Leon Oberman painting?" Matilde's voice squeaked, aghast.

Hesper couldn't explain what came over her. She'd just met this woman. And God only knew what Matilde thought of her. But she felt absolute certainty that Matilde had felt genuine affection for Leon. How sad was it that no one who had really known the man, really loved him, had seen the paintings into which he'd poured so much of his soul?

Everyone deserved to be seen.

"This is going to sound crazy, but would you like to come out and see them? It's hard to explain, but I'd like for someone who actually knew him to see what I've seen."

"Are you kidding? I would drive a thousand miles to see a new Leon Oberman. This is all I have left: his other works sold and went to help cover his estate's expenses soon after his death."

Hesper wrote down her address and the driving instructions.

"I hope you won't feel anxious driving out in the middle

of nowhere to come to a stranger's house. It's just me and my husband Richard out there. And he's an elementary school music teacher, so you can't really find anyone less threatening than that."

Matilde laughed. "I'm a pretty good judge of character. You have to be in Santa Fe. Don't be fooled by all the trappings. It looks like a big city, but it operates like a small town. Honestly, I can't tell you how excited I am to see more of Leon's work. Is the day after tomorrow too soon for you?"

"Not at all. I'll be out there all day, so just show up whenever it works for you."

On a whim, Hesper walked over to the gift shop a few doors down and bought a couple of red chili pepper strings before getting back in her car. They'd look perfect on either side of her front door. Richard would tease her, no doubt, for being such a stereotypical white girl, but she didn't care. The bright crimson cheered her somehow. And the idea of having someone who'd known Leon personally seeing the paintings locked away in cupboards and cabinets felt like redemption. This was a good thing, she was sure.

She'd promised herself to get her hair done, too, hadn't she? She spotted a day spa that looked promising and pulled in.

The place smelled of lavender and sage and dyeing chemicals. Silk curtains and dark umber walls lent luxury and indulgence to the mood. A young girl in a short black dress looked up as Hesper entered.

"Can I help you?"

"I need a cut and color. Can I make an appointment?"

"Oh. I can schedule you next week if you like, but we actually just had a cancellation with Amber. There's time to do it now, if you'd rather."

Hesper hesitated. She hadn't been prepared for a salon appointment right this minute. She wasn't even entirely sure she'd made up her mind what she wanted. But maybe spontaneity was good. Besides, who knew how hard it would be to convince herself to leave the house some day next week?

She was on a roll. She'd met with eight galleries, made appointments with five, and left her portfolio with the other three. Not to mention her encounter with Matilde. She might as well make it a banner day. Maybe new hair could be her reward for being a grown up all mastodon-munching day.

"You know what?" she decided aloud. "Right now sounds perfect. Thank you."

But when she saw Amber *(were all hair stylists named Amber?)* walking toward her with an easy smile, her heart sank.

Maybe twenty-five years old, Amber wore a silver smock over a black dress nearly identical to the hostess's. Glancing around, Hesper realized all the stylists were dressed in the same fashion. Unlike the overworked, fried hair Hesper often saw sported at less pricey salons, Amber's hair was a beautiful shining gold shot through with subtle platinum accents, falling in soft waves around her heart-shaped face. Wire-rimmed silver glasses gave her a charmingly owlish look.

She looked familiar. Very, very familiar. Hesper's feet felt rooted to the floor.

"Hello, Hesper? I'm Amber. Let's get you to a shampoo station, and we can discuss what you'd like done today."

Much to her dismay, Hesper's body propelled itself forward, seemingly of its own volition. Amber led the way to a cushy leather seat, settling Hesper's neck onto a plush towel as she gently pulled her hair back into the sink. Somehow this spa had found the ever-elusive equation of comfort and efficiency so that Hesper actually didn't feel like her neck was going to snap in two while Amber's expert fingers massaged the lightly scented shampoo into her hair.

Even Amber's voice was soothingly low-pitched. Hesper hated it.

"Monica said you were looking for a cut and color. What can I do for you today?"

Hesper struggled to sound casual. Normal. Not like a woman about to have a full-on panic attack.

"How about an all-over copper color, with some platinum lowlights? And just a trim up on the cut, more of the same shaggy layers."

"No problem." Amber's strong fingers moved down her neck and over her shoulders in a light massage that felt impossibly good. God, how long had it been since someone touched her? Really touched her? Couldn't people go mad for lack of touch? Hesper thought she'd read something about that.

Why did Amber have to look just like Libby? *Why?*

She'd tried so hard to forget Libby entirely. She squeezed her lids shut, tried to pretend the chemical fumes were burning her eyes.

CHAPTER ELEVEN

Hesper couldn't have recalled a single detail from the drive home if she'd been put under hypnosis. The road flew away beneath her tires, and it was some kind of miracle the cops didn't pull her over, at the speeds she was going. Maybe it wasn't a miracle. More likely than angels looking after her was the devil himself clearing the way. After all, heaven hadn't been on her side for a long while now, had it?

Her traitorous body was a mass of contradictory sensations. The botanical-scented hair chemicals filled the car with a peace-inducing aromatherapy, a peace Hesper resisted with every cell. Her head felt light, her muscles teased into something almost like pleasure. Almost, because a crawling contempt ran counter to the delight, a horrified shock that she'd even allowed that woman to touch her.

Hesper shook her head violently and had to fight to pull the car out of a swerve. Heated desert air blew like a sirocco through the car, every window rolled down. Amber *wasn't* that woman, though. Hesper's stupid brain was confusing her. Amber wasn't Libby. She was just some sweet aesthetician with an unfortunate resemblance to the woman Richard had been sleeping with in Evanston.

She howled at the brutal thought, stuffing a fist in her mouth to muffle the sound.

She'd tried so hard to forget, to push all memories of that

woman out of her mind. And most of the time, she succeeded. It wasn't as if Richard would ever betray her again. There was no wisdom or happiness to be found holding onto old hurts. Consigning Libby Lyons to the void where she belonged was the best thing Hesper could do for herself. And for Richard.

It wasn't as if Libby hadn't known Richard was married, after all. Quite the contrary. She'd been his solace, his confidante, his refuge against the dry misery of his marriage. She deserved to be forgotten. To be unnamed. To be *nothing*. Hesper laughed bitterly, the sound maniacal in her own ears.

Pretty little empty-headed elementary school teacher. How much more disgustingly sweet could Libby have possibly been? With her soft blond curls and bubble-gum lipstick and whispery little giggles. She'd had none of Hesper's hard edges. The fiercest passion that drove Libby had probably been completing her lesson plans by summer's end.

Even while shocked at the dark turn of her own thoughts, Hesper couldn't help taking a grim, black satisfaction in what had to be the other woman's misery now. We all reap what we sow, don't we? she thought bitterly. She herself had reaped the whirlwind, and there was no escaping the hot gales that daily scoured the flesh from her brittle, aching bones. But pretty little Libby bore a suffering of her own, and Hesper was fiercely glad for it.

The Subaru was too good a performer to screech its way into the drive, but a cloud of dust covered the car as she threw it into park and stepped out.

"Richard!" she yelled as she stormed toward the house. "Richard!"

She flung open the door. The house was quiet and dim, the only sound was the fans humming as they kept the air flowing. Richard appeared from the hallway, as if he'd been in the studio when she drove up.

Licorice sticks, but she still loved him so much. Her mouth went dry at the sight of him there, all but transparent in the shadowy half-light. His dark hair fell disheveled over his glasses, his square jaw dusted with scruff. His shoulders were broad, and she knew well how strong his arms were under the unassuming plaid button-down shirt he wore. His soft belly made her want to wrap her arms fiercely around his midsection and bury her head against his chest and never let him go. His gaze as his eyes met hers was mild, vaguely troubled at the tempest on her face but laced with the steadiest of affections.

"What's wrong, Hesper?"

Her hands balled into fists at her side.

"I'm so, so angry."

"Tell me about it." He crossed into the kitchen, retrieving a cider from the fridge for her and setting it on the table. He folded his long legs under the bench seat on his side and nodded for her to take a seat. She willed her taut muscles to cooperate and sat down, feeling as if every movement were about to break a bone.

"It's me you're angry at, isn't it?" he prompted her gently.

"Yes. No. I'm not angry at you. I'm angry at her. I'm angry at what happened. I'm angry, so angry, at myself."

She didn't even taste the cider as it bubbled down her throat. Richard reached across the table and took her hands in his.

"Hesper, you're angry at me."

She shook her head, hard.

"I'm angry at you," he said confidingly, almost tenderly. "Is that allowed?"

"Of course you're angry at me."

"Not about the accident."

"Then what?" She raised her head and searched his eyes warily.

"Don't misunderstand me. What I did was wrong. My choices are all mine alone to bear. But I didn't act in a vacuum."

"What do you mean? I would have never cheated on you."

"No?" He smiled crookedly. "Maybe not with another man or woman. Or honestly, you might have done that too and not even registered the act yourself. You were a thousand miles away from our marriage, and you had been for a very long time."

Fury speared through Hesper's belly. "So, because I cared about something besides you, I deserved to be cheated on? If you aren't the center of the universe, you have no choice but to prop your wee little male ego up with some sex on the side? Why must you be so pathetically petted all the time?"

Richard let go of her hands and leaned back. "You're the one who wants to hear the truth now. Can you listen, or can you only attack still?"

"You're sitting there telling me you abandoned our marriage because I was distracted. By my career."

"That's not what I'm saying at all, Hesper. And I think you know me much, much better than that. Nobody on this earth knows me better than you do. I'm saying I was lonely. I'd been lonely for years."

"Years?" Hesper's throat hurt.

"Do you remember our three-year plan?"

"So now this is about me not wanting to be a baby machine?"

Richard sighed. "I'm not your enemy. We can't get anywhere with each other if you turn every statement I make into an attack."

"It is, though, isn't it?"

Finally, a spark of anger flared in Richard's blue eyes. "It isn't. But you wouldn't even talk to me about it. When we got married, we made all our plans together. We talked about our dreams and plotted out all sorts of ways to get there.

Then all of a sudden, you started making our decisions all by yourself. You didn't want to explain what had changed or where we were headed. If I had to give up all my dreams of being a father altogether or if we were just delaying the plan. You became a mystery. My own future became a mystery I wasn't allowed to question."

Hesper pictured Richard holding an infant of his own, cradling the baby close to his face, and her bones ached. "I'm sorry," she whispered. "I didn't know you felt like that."

"I tried to tell you," Richard said flatly. "But I don't want you to be sorry. I want to know why. Did you not want a family anymore? Was the whole idea just a curse, a burden on you as an artist? Or was it me you didn't want as a father to your children?"

"As an artist?" Hesper echoed derisively, dropping her face back into her hands. "That was the whole problem, Richard. Never you. I was a complete fraud, and I knew it. I'd been an idiot when we got married, and I really thought three years would be plenty of time for me to establish myself in the Chicago scene. I didn't think I'd be a big deal yet, obviously, but I thought I'd at least be a regular. People would know my name. People would buy my pots. I'd be helping to support our family, instead of just constantly draining it."

"But you had gallery shows all the time. And you even won those awards. The Trib' ran that big story on you."

Her mouth twisted. "Smoke and mirrors. It looks good from the outside, but it didn't mean anything. Not really. I was still lucky if I broke even buying supplies. I sure wasn't contributing to our retirement in the Cayman Islands."

"I wish you'd told me you were feeling like a failure."

Hesper drew a deep, shaky breath.

"I wish I had, too."

"I thought you despised me. I was too mundane, too bourgeois for the artist's life you craved. What kind of conversations could an artist have with a schoolteacher? Almost none, anymore. All we talked about was errands and bills. When we did have sex, it felt like you were doing me a reluctant favor."

"You definitely never tried to tell me that."

"No." Richard shook his head. "Eventually I didn't want to hear the truth from you anymore. As long as I didn't corner you into telling me what you were feeling, I could pretend we still had a chance at making it through whatever was happening to us. You got quiet, and I let you. I was a coward."

"But how could we make it through if you went to someone else instead?" This time Hesper spoke sincerely, her question aching with confusion, not accusation.

Richard shrugged. "Desperation, Hesper. You're not wrong to think me small, I guess. Pathetic. I'd have never left you. But to feel needed? Wanted, really wanted, for a minute.

Just plain liked. That was my drug. I could forget how lonely I was for a bit. I could feel like I was enough for someone. I could believe I'd be enough for you again, one day."

The words sat between them for a long while.

"I don't want to think about this anymore," Hesper said miserably. More than anything, she wanted to tell Richard he was all she needed in life, but even now, she knew that wasn't true. If she could undo everything that happened that night six months ago, and all she had to give up was the clay, she wouldn't do it. And she hated, *hated* that about herself. But there was no herself outside of that truth.

"I wouldn't want you to," Richard said softly, and Hesper imagined he was responding not to what she'd said, but to what she'd thought. She rubbed her eyes wearily.

Glancing over at him, she muffled a scream and turned away, curling into herself. Richard rose with a clatter, crossing swiftly to wrap his arms around her shoulders. "What is it? What is it, Hesper?"

She shook, clutching at him, her eyes searching his as he lifted her head. "That horrible dream. Sometimes I have it even when I'm awake."

Just for an instant, that dreadful image of tree limb and windshield glass and Richard's shattered head had superimposed over him as he'd sat there across from her. Every night, she dreaded closing her eyes, but now even the sunlight offered no sure respite.

Maybe Ginny and Richard were right. Maybe she should start taking her pills again.

No. She could only lose so much of herself.

"I'm sorry, sweet." Richard rubbed her back. "You should eat something."

Hesper nodded meekly. As she went through the motions of filling a plate with God-only-knew-what, her mind ran over and over the words Richard had spoken. How dearly she wished they hadn't hurt each other so deeply. Maybe it had all been inevitable. However Richard might wish it was otherwise, she'd always known she had something cold and hard at her center. Something that would forever push the art ahead of everything else. Maybe even if she'd admitted how she'd been feeling, that coldness would still have doomed them. Maybe Richard's need for affirmation meant he'd have always looked elsewhere in the end, regardless. Maybe, as much as it hurt, his wandering had been the best thing he could have done, for them both.

She didn't really believe any of that. But accepting that events didn't have to unfold exactly as they had was sadder and more awful than she could bear right now.

She stole a glance at her husband. Seemingly untroubled by the conversation they'd just had, he sat absorbed in a paperback novel, his glasses slipping down his nose, his hair shadowing his cheek. She watched as the emotions on the page played over his unguarded face. He was just along for the ride, somehow, she supposed. He would always let her take it as far as she could and no further. In the strangest way, she was spoiled. Placated and pandered.

She took her plate to the recliner, flipping up the footrest and starting her true crime documentaries. In spite of how their conversation had knotted her up in the most agonizing of ways, she felt more at peace than she had in months. Almost as if this wound might heal, after all. They'd never been able to talk through the infidelity and what had become of their marriage. That one dreadful "conversation," which had consisted of her screaming and crying as she fought to control the car on those icy early spring roads, with a white-faced Richard frantically apologizing and trying to convince her to pull over, had been their singular effort at facing the truth. They'd never dared broach the subject since.

Now, the pain running through her veins felt almost like love itself. She hugged the words he'd said to her body: "Nobody on this earth knows me better than you do."

That was something, wasn't it? Surely there was no greater gift any soul could offer another than to hold the knowledge of them, whole and sacrosanct, against all the inroads and corruption of life.

"I do know you, Richard," she whispered. On the computer screen in front of her, an actor struggled to lift the carpet-wrapped body of his wife into the back of their minivan. "I won't let you go."

CHAPTER TWELVE

Hesper started in the chair, her hands scrabbling automatically to catch the plate and laptop before they went careening to the floor. Her fork escaped and fell with a clatter that made her ears ring. What had woken her?

Sweat soaked her hair. She blinked in the darkness, trying to make sense of the sensation and adjust to the faint moonlight.

The windows were closed, the fans off.

Gingerly she lowered the recliner to its sitting position and unfolded her stiff body from its buttery leather. She set her computer and plate in the seat of the chair and pivoted.

The silence in the house was oppressive. She had the strangest idea, that the universe had compressed and squeezed this space in on itself, that it existed forever and entirely apart from the rest of reality. Outside, she could hear a high wind whipping through the trees, their long, crazy-armed shadows danced eerily upon the walls and floor. She crossed to the window and raised its glass, looking out.

Oh, she did not like that. The eerie aggression of the tree-shadows was a thousand times worse when viewed from here, their black figures lashing and dashing toward and over the house again and again. She shuddered.

Behind her, she heard a soft snick. Then another. And another.

Holding her breath, she turned. For a moment, everything looked the same. Then movement caught her eye.

One by one, the kitchen cabinet doors were opening. The many faces of Leon Oberman's son stared at her. *Andrew.* Andy Oberman. She'd finally done her research last night, before she fell asleep. The child had been named Andy.

The multitude of expressions Leon Oberman had captured in his paintings all coalesced now into one. Menace.

Cold, unadulterated menace.

"Why?" she mumbled, clutching at her t-shirt as if it offered some sort of defense. Why did he hate her so much? She hadn't done anything to him.

Not to *him*, came a cold little voice in her brain. But you're no innocent.

Down the hallway, she could hear the sound of the bathroom cabinet and the closet door creaking open. She wasn't even sure if they creaked normally, but somehow or other, she could hear them opening now.

Goosebumps swept over her skin. Her breathing was all wrong: too fast, too slow, coming in jerks and starts. A child's voice rose off-key in lilting song.

"You are my sunshine, my only sunshine..."

Hesper clapped her hands over her ears. One of the cabinet doors slammed shut and bounced back open. She shrieked. Another slammed. Another.

All together, in some gruesome chorus, they slammed

shut. Opened. Slammed shut. Opened. The booming percussion was deafening.

Something was coming for her. Terror burned through her veins. She felt capillaries splitting. The pounding grew faster and faster.

She broke free of whatever spell had held her immobilized and ran for the front door, snatching her keys with nerveless fingers from their hook. Her bare feet skidded to a stop on the cold dry earth, unmindful of the cacti tearing at her ankle.

"Nonononono..."

A massive tree limb was imbedded in the passenger side of her car windshield. Something pushed her forward. Red and blue lights from nowhere played crazily over the shattered glass, almost but not quite illuminating what lay beneath.

The keys dropped from her hand.

Sobbing, she tore herself free of whatever force impelled her and ran around the courtyard wall, away from the house, away from the crushed car, toward the little wood. The wind that tore and twisted the trees snatched at her hair and whipped tears from her eyes. She could see the heavy, sheet-wrapped clay swinging from the branch on which it was tied. Perched on the limb, its legs split over the heavy knot, the shadow-boy peered down at her.

Those eyes. All light, fiery, prisming light holding a

thousand colors yet somehow burning pure white. Light was supposed to be good, wasn't it? But the only thing Hesper found more terrifying than the boy's eyes was its mouth.

Or rather, its lack of a mouth. Seamless darkness stretched beneath those abyss eyes into an awful chin-face. Still, somehow, she could hear it laughing.

"What do you want?" she cried.

The boy shook his head and pointed.

Hesper hadn't thought she could feel any greater fear, but dread bubbled up as she turned with agonizing slowness.

Across the clearing, under the trees on the other side, Hesper saw Leon Oberman. She had no doubt it was him. She just knew.

He stared at her, his dark eyes gaping. In spite of herself, she felt her feet lifting, crossing the distance between them. She expected him to become transparent as she approached, but if anything, he became more corporeal, more solid. More undeniable. She stopped about six feet away.

The awful menace and hatred she'd felt in the house was gone. Leon Oberman posed no threat to her, she was sure. If anything, they were connected, by what cord she didn't know. Wouldn't admit. Sadness poured over him, so hot and thick she coughed. She reached for him.

He was so terribly, terribly alone.

He kept his hands at his sides. "I'm sorry," he mouthed.

He vanished.

The wind died in a whoosh, the trees pulling themselves erect with what she swore was relief. Hesper spun around and squinted through the darkness toward her clay-hanging tree. The shadow-boy was gone.

Every muscle in her body quivered as if it had been pushed past exhaustion. She stumbled across the yard and crept around the courtyard wall, willing herself not to flinch as she looked toward her little Subaru, parked in the driveway.

Not so much as a tree branch or a pine needle lay on its hood. The windshield stretched unbroken and dark. Relief shuddered through her.

The front door hung open as she'd left it. She reached around the doorjamb with shaking fingers and flipped the light switch before stepping through. Closing the door softly behind her, she stretched her neck to peep into the kitchen, but her caution was unnecessary. All the cabinets were shut fast. No hint of what had happened remained.

If it had happened at all, her mind hissed at her.

She tiptoed through the rest of the house, turning on every light as she went. She wasn't sure what she was looking for, but at any rate, she found nothing at all. The closets, too, were closed. Richard's desk was undisturbed, his papers secured from the wind with heavy books. Even the bathroom felt entirely ordinary. The empty mirror frame seemed neglected rather than leering.

The only light she left off was the one in her own bedroom. If Richard had managed to sleep through all her hysteria, there was no reason to wake him now. She undressed down to her panties and crawled into the cool sheets, trying not to disturb the mattress. But Richard reached for her right away, his strong arms pulling her back against his bare chest.

"Shhh," he murmured, as if he knew everything. "It's only a dream. This, right here, is what's real. Me and you. Everything else is a dream."

CHAPTER THIRTEEN

Hesper didn't recognize the number on her phone and almost ignored it. When she answered it, she wished she'd followed her first instinct.

"Ms. Dunn? This is Hank with Glass Solutions. We were able to get your mirror done a couple days early, if you'd like to go ahead and pick it up. It'll be ready whenever you are."

Ugh. She'd been looking forward to spending the day at home. She felt like she'd done nothing but run errands since she moved here. So much for her dream of disappearing into the sand. No doubt it was good for mental health to keep moving, but it felt about as good as broccoli tasted.

Still, the sooner she got things in order, the sooner she could relax and settle into a regular schedule. And Matilde would probably be coming out tomorrow, so she might as well get this over with today. Then she could dedicate some time to simply be in this place and really get into the clay. She didn't know what her next piece was going to be yet, but she'd never find out if she didn't let the inspiration bubble and simmer untroubled for a while.

Listening. Listening and looking were the key skills of any artist. Unbidden, the image of the Lady playing her weird little organ in the garden rose to Hesper's mind. No wonder the Lady looked so unhappy in that piece. Rather than be allowed to listen to the birds singing and the wind blowing through the fruit trees, she was required to perform something completely foreign and other from her environment. How dangerous it might have been to the establishment, had they allowed her peace and time to listen to the free air.

Still, the Lady had found her way out, hadn't she? Or at least Hesper liked to think so. She found she was more fascinated by the ancient story told on tapestry than she'd expected to be. She hadn't thought she'd have anything in common with some noble character from another continent and culture, hadn't expected to feel kinship with the stitched eyes and somber mouth. But the little tableaus had drawn her in. Hesper felt invested in what became of the Lady and her Unicorn, as if it weren't a story hundreds of years old. As if it were unfolding now, each conflict and decision resolved only as Hesper perceived them and not before.

Taste would be next. Maybe when she got home with the mirror, she'd spend a little time there. A funny anticipation perked in her tummy. She looked forward to losing herself in the threads. It was almost like reading a really good book. Foreshadowing and subplots hidden everywhere in the field of flowers. Compelling characters and the highest of stakes—happiness.

One of Hesper's favorite things about the Subie was its fuel efficiency, but even so, she needed to remember to get gas while she was in town. All these treks back and forth were draining her tank. Soon enough, she'd put herself on a once-a-week schedule. She'd pick a day when she could make the gallery rounds, buy groceries, maybe even force herself to sit in a coffee shop for a while like a normal person. If she was going to make this her home, then she had to make these her people, too. And there was no fast track, no magic method to that.

Just like the clay they were made of, people required time.

Maybe since she was going to be in town anyway, she'd grab some doughnuts while she gassed up. Doughnuts made any journey worthwhile, didn't they? And it would be fitting for her perusal of *Taste*. Hesper grinned. Justification of sugar and fat was a particular skill of hers. In this case, the art demanded it. Obviously. She thought Ginny would approve of her philosophical edict.

The whole diversion only took a couple hours. By the time she was back at home, the Subaru was full of gas, her fingers were sticky, and her belly was bursting. She could have waited till she got home to start on her delectable breakfast, but why delay pleasure? She still had one more doughnut she could eat later, while musing over whatever dilemma the Lady faced in her current panel.

But for now—she washed her hands in the kitchen sink and dried them briskly. She dug a pair of thick leather gloves out of the hall closet for handling the mirror. They'd been

Richard's, and they were a little big on her. She slid her sluggish fingers deliberately into the stiff, cool cloth, squeezing her hands into gentle fists as if she could feel Richard's hands in hers. She'd have to be careful: her hands still didn't always respond as deftly as she wanted them to.

The glass company had been conscientious about how they wrapped the mirror, framing it with cardboard and foam and packing tape. If it broke, it would be her own fault. She braced herself before hefting its weight out of the hatchback and carrying it into the house. She took it into the bathroom and set it carefully against the wall, wedging its base against the foot of the toilet so it wouldn't slide.

With the help of a stepladder, she determined the frame was the simplest possible design. Basically a narrow box, open at the top, into which she could slide the glass. The only trick would be controlling the speed of the mirror as it lowered so that it didn't bang into place and shatter. Although, the glass was actually quite thick. She suspected it would not be so easy to break a mirror as she feared.

The last thing she needed was seven years of bad luck, so she intended to be very, very careful all the same.

Seven years. The length of a marriage. The length of a lifetime together.

Standing on the stepladder, she stroked the bare wood of the empty frame. Only a few days, and she'd already gotten weirdly used to its blank face. It was as if that long street of memories Leon Oberman had shown her that night still hummed and breathed there, just past her perception. She thought of a young struggling father, of the joy in his eyes when he looked at his son, of the closeness of a small sweaty hand clasped in his. Part of her didn't want to cover that wood up with a glass that did not reveal but only reflected.

Hesper smiled self-deprecatingly. What a whimsical thought. What she'd seen hadn't been real in the first place. Only the product of her too-fertile imagination, fed by half-stories from the realtor and the paintings Leon himself had left behind as his legacy. Certainly she wasn't silencing them by replacing a broken mirror.

Taking a deep breath, she raised the heavy weight of the glass over her head and fitted it into the box of the frame. Once she had it lowered halfway, she braced one hand against its surface to slow its descent as she held on to the top of the mirror as tightly as she could. She gritted her teeth and focused intently on the tension in her fingers. *Hold, hold, hold.* A soft thud. The glass fit perfectly into place.

"Rather anticlimactic," she said, shaking out her hands. "Anticlimactic is good. Definitely beats my normal of melodramatic hysteria."

She grabbed the window cleaner from under the sink and wiped away the smears. Her own face gazed back at her. Her eyes, even under the makeup, were puffy and shadowed.

Unsurprising, considering the nights she'd been having. But her new haircut flattered her bone structure, and its striking colors lent her more vitality than she was sure she had.

"Just a regular mirror, after all."

Unable to resist, she pulled open the cabinet door and examined the face of the little boy painted there. No menace, no hostility glittered in the strokes of paint now. If anything, affection swelled unexpectedly in her chest.

"Hello, Andy. I think we would've been friends, don't you?"

She closed the door, feeling somber but not sad. She gathered up the packing debris from the mirror and carried it outside to the covered trash bins. The design was efficient, with locking doors and lids. The rubbish would be easy to retrieve when she was ready to haul it into town, but in the meantime, wildlife couldn't access it. She didn't think bears came down this far into the desert, but there were plenty of other critters to discourage.

Hesper grabbed her last doughnut—a chocolate-covered cruller with sprinkles—and a cider and retreated into the cool dimness of the living room. Outside the heat was already oppressive. The fans, placed at the windows, kept the house cool and refreshing. Not the same as air conditioning, but Hesper found herself oddly reluctant to try out the swamp cooler attached to her bedroom. She was enjoying the sensation of an intimate connection with nature and its cycles. She didn't want to insulate herself from that.

Not yet, anyway.

She adjusted the recliner to directly face the tapestry wall and settled into its leathery embrace with a satisfied sigh.

"What story do you have to tell me today, Lady?"

Her teeth sank into the cruller. To her happy surprise, the cheap gas station pastry had somehow managed to escape the fate of most mass-produced crullers. Rather than collapsing into grease-sodden goo, the spiral walls of the cruller were wonderfully crisp, the interior melting in her mouth. Chocolate frosting crowned the whole affair with delectable decadence.

"Nice dress you've got there, Lady, but I would take this cruller over any number of jewels."

And it was a very nice dress. Maybe the most elaborate of any of the panels.

The Lady's veil fluttered in the wind, but rather than lending a sense of freedom and vitality to the image, the contrast between the coursing of the breeze and the stiffness of the Lady was heightened. Leaning forward to examine it more closely, Hesper saw what looked like a little dog sat on the train of that oh-so-fancy dress.

That made sense, thought Hesper. Dogs represented loyalty, didn't they? Fidelity? The Lady was held captive, serving the hungers of others, by her loyalty to the very system that kept her imprisoned in a garden. A garden bounded in this panel by thorny rose bushes. Not terribly subtle, that.

The dour-faced lady-in-waiting held a tray of sweets from which the Lady fed a golden bird. Hesper liked to think that the artist intended for the close eye to understand that though she might have been confined by thorns and held fast by a fidelity she hadn't chosen, she did not neglect to feed her longings for freedom. What she could not taste herself, she fed to the creature who could leave the garden and bring back news of the world beyond. Already the Lady plotted her escape.

The positions of the Lion and the Unicorn in this panel were baffling. The Lion stood rampant as he held his pennant aloft, his eyes fixed on the lady, his tail whipping, his teeth snarling. Was he angry that she fed her flyaway hope? Or was his fury on her behalf, his ire roused by her capture and forced servitude?

The Unicorn formed a counterpart to the Lion, his own pennant equally bold, but rather than observe the Lady, his head was turned over his shoulder, his gaze cast behind him, beyond the garden border. Perhaps he could not bear to see her humbled so. He disdained even to watch her offer delights to others which she herself was not permitted to indulge. Or was he distracted by something outside their tableau? Some danger, or else some promise? Hesper liked the disparity, the discord, in the responses of the Lady's defenders. Whatever was happening within the garden island, they were torn, fraught, discontented. And what was more human than that?

Do people ever really know what they want in life? When they had it, they discounted and neglected it. And when they sought it, how often did they turn back before the prize was secured, so easily dissuaded by difficulty and cost. The *Taste* panel seemed to her an illumination of the restlessness and vexation that typified human struggle. At the Lady's feet crouched a merry little monkey who had plainly stolen one of the sweets for himself. His was the only happy face in the entire scene.

Given the medieval emphasis on symbolism and penchant for layers upon layers of allegory, Hesper didn't imagine for an instant any of the details of the tapestries were accidental. The artist would have known very well all the questions he was raising, the controversial stories he concealed in every corner of his images. Perhaps even the very colors held a hidden message. And yet he'd managed to pull it all off in what would have been one of the most expensive commissions of its day. Pretty and pastoral, but only to the shallowest of gazes. Anyone who looked a moment longer saw so much more.

A secret rebel, Hesper thought, hidden in plain sight.

As if summoned by the object of her attention, Hesper's

phone rang. She glanced at the screen.

Ginny.

Hesper silenced the call. She'd ignored Ginny's calls for a couple of days now. Ginny was insightful. Intuitive. Downright shrewd. If Hesper spoke to her, she'd know something was up. And what could Hesper tell her? *My house is haunted. I'm haunted.*

Ginny would just start harping on the meds again. Hesper had come out here with the intention of opening herself up and listening to all the spirits and forces in this place. Her brain might be taking that a bit far, fabricating dramas in an effort to understand the beings who had once called the desert home.

It didn't feel imaginary, though. She was sure she'd been wide awake last night. But what evidence did she have of that? Not a thing was out of place now. The paintings looked just the same as they always had. That powerful sense of hatred and loathing that had all but choked her last night was gone, as if it had never been. Her home smelled fresh and wild, its confines peaceful and content.

Ginny would want her to come back to Evanston, to move in with her and Felka. How many times had she argued for that very thing? But leaving wasn't an option. This was Hesper's home. As it had been Leon Oberman's home.

That didn't feel eerie or ominous to Hesper. Art, love, grief—all these left indelible marks on any environment they breathed. Leon had suffered here, but suffering was life. He had also created here, powerful and evocative works. His sadness echoed, as did his sense of beauty.

There was a completeness to it. Not a closing of the circle, but a pursuit of the snake's tail. Infinite creation, bound up in the periodic of good-byes.

Still, Hesper did feel a little guilty. Ginny would worry. She would send her a quick email, tell her she was busy, but she was okay. That should hold her off for a while.

Now, if Hesper could just get through this evening and night without her brain playing any more projectionist's tricks. Not that Hesper was convinced it was all in her head.

She didn't believe for a minute that the shadow-child was actually Andy Oberman, as much as its silhouette was clearly patterned after him. What child, especially one whose innocence would have never expired, would be filled with such incredible hatred? Even if his father could somehow be counted responsible for his son's death, Hesper was sure it hadn't been a deliberate act. Andy wouldn't have wanted to torture and torment his father. Leon did that to himself.

Based on the street of memories Leon Oberman had showed her in the mirror frame that night, she simply didn't believe death would have changed that loving, sweet little boy into an imp, a cruel demon whose only intent was harm. Something else had to be at play.

"Leon?" she whispered on a whim. "Are you here?"

The melodious quiet of the desert remained as it had been: the rustling of leaves, the humming of the fans, the occasional chirrup of a lizard.

Hesper's lips twisted. How silly was she? Still, she tried again.

"Leon? I know the shadow-boy isn't Andy. What is it? What does it want?"

She jerked painfully as a sudden whirring sound erupted from down the hall. She ran into the studio, her heart pounding. Her wheel spun at high speed in the empty room.

"Richard?" she called automatically, but there was no answer. She yanked the cord out of the wall, and the wheel slowed to a stop. One after another, the buckets of clay lined up under the shelves tipped over.

"Stop it," she said as firmly as she could, though her knees quaked. "This is my studio. My space. You don't belong here. Leave us alone."

She wasn't sure if by us, she meant herself and Richard or herself and Leon Oberman. Maybe both.

"You are my sunshine, my only sunshine..."

"Sing all you want. This house is mine now. You aren't going to chase me away. You can't hurt me."

No sooner had the words left her mouth, than she regretted them.

CHAPTER FOURTEEN

The inevitability of darkness in the desert that night felt particularly oppressive. Hesper stayed outside as night fell, oddly reluctant to close herself within the walls of the house. She'd intended to wait a couple more days before working with her foot-powered wheel, but after the incident in her studio, she needed to ground herself somehow.

She'd tugged the heavy buckets of clay back into their upright positions and secured them with a loading strap so they couldn't be tipped over again. She left her wheel unplugged and closed the window, as if that futile gesture could keep anything out. She closed the door, too, unsure if she meant to keep something out or to keep something in.

She'd even gone and stared into the bathroom mirror, but all she saw there was her own wild-eyed face. What kind of manic person thought it was a good idea to taunt a ghost?

Restless and out-of-sorts and ill-at-ease, she'd resorted to her clay, as she always did. A fine sheen of perspiration cooled on her skin as the shadows lengthened and took on a purple hue. Her fingers worked ceaselessly, meeting and matching and finally mastering the rhythms of the clay. The stiffness of her damaged hands seemed to fall away, but in truth, she was only incorporating her new, aborted movements into the old cadences of memory. Power rippled through her arms, her shoulders, her back. Her thighs squeezed and her foot pumped a percussive song of creation.

The fear and anxiety that had briefly choked her had dissipated. The act of throwing a new pot, here in the courtyard, in the style of her ancestors, reclaimed the property. Whatever thought to walk here, she was the one with flesh and bones. She was the one with life. That shadow-child and its malice wanted something from her, that was clear. Which meant she was the one in the position of power. She was stronger than whatever black energy fed its spirit. That was what she told herself, anyway.

Still, she didn't like to see the retreat of the sun, the wild unfurling of colors across the empty sky. All around the house, the ring of trees swayed and bowed with the advent of the evening wind. Hesper imagined they warned her: *get inside, get inside.*

She bent nearer to her pot, as if she could hoard the last remnants of light between her belly and her hands. Pour it over the lip of the pot and carry it with her through the night.

It did not work. The sun flamed out with a flamboyant burst of violet-tinged orange, and then all was grey. The trees, the house, the earth, even her own hands, were grey. And something darker roiled across the desert plains apace.

A weird panic seized her, and her hands slipped on the wire as she pulled the pot from the wheel, transferring it to a board to carry it back to the shelves in her studio. The kiln that had felt all evening like a companion now loomed grim and unfriendly from the edge of the flagstones. *It's watching me*, she thought, as she hobbled into the house with her burden. Hungry for flames, hungry for sacrifices born of earth and blood.

The house, she could tell, had been waiting for her to come back in. Its quiet stillness whooshed around her, enveloping her as she kicked the door closed behind her. She had no hands free to switch on the lights, so she walked down the hall in darkness, already well familiar with the layout of the house.

She used her elbow to lever the doorknob, crossing the room as quickly as she could to deposit her pot on a shelf for drying. The room was uncomfortably hot and stuffy—her own fault, for closing the window and the door. She turned back with a rush of terror and flipped the light on, her eyes darting to every corner.

It was empty, of course. What had she expected? She leaned over Richard's desk and flung open the window, switching on the fan to blow out the heat.

Behind her, the door began to close.

She spun around, seizing the edge of the door just before it snicked shut. She tugged, but something tugged back.

"Who's there?" she quavered. She strained to see into the darkness on the other side, but it was as if the light from the studio simply stopped at the edge of the door. Perfect darkness breathed in the hall. Darkness, and something else.

Maybe she shouldn't be fighting to open the door at all. Maybe she should slam it shut and keep whatever was out there firmly on the other side.

But *it* had wanted her locked in here, so that alone was reason enough to fight. Her muscles, already tired from her hours at the wheel, screamed as she braced her feet and pulled with all her might.

With agonizing slowness, the door crept in her direction. She wedged a bare foot against the bottom. Edging her weight into the opening, she put her back against the doorjamb and propelled herself into the hallway. The door slammed shut behind her.

"*My studio*," a taunting voice she recognized too well echoed her earlier words.

Fury, welcome in its fearlessness, roared into her veins.

"It is not!" she yelled back at the door. "This is *my* studio. This is my house. This is my home. You are the interloper. You do not belong!"

Her stomach dropped as she heard the sound of shattering ceramic. She seized the door handle, but it wouldn't turn.

Another crash.

"No!"

She threw her body against the door, but it barely registered the force. "Stop it!"

Crash.

The destruction taking place on the other side sounded unhurried, even casual. Hesper beat and pounded until her hands were raw. There were only so many pots to break. The crashing subsided into what sounded like someone lazily kicking the broken shards across the floor. Hesper slid down the door, sobbing as she dropped her head between her knees.

"It's my studio. Mine."

The kicking continued, an eerily playful sound.

"You know what?" Hesper raised her head. "You're just angry because you can't make anything. All you can do is destroy. Tear down. Break things. You're not powerful. You're the opposite of power."

The doorknob over her head turned, and she fell backward with a shriek as the door shot open.

The light was still on. Hesper scrambled to her knees but got no farther as her damp gaze traveled the room. "Ham sandwiches," she breathed. "You filthy mastodon-muncher."

Her pots weren't just broken, they were obliterated. Dust and tiny shards covered the floor and coated the shelves. She couldn't even identify a curl of root or a bit of branch from her beloved World Tree collection. And the lovely massive pot she'd begun just tonight lay smashed and stomped into a formless heap.

Her tears dried up. Sorrow, rage, terror, all abandoned

her. She was only empty now.

Shaking, she rose to her feet and then collapsed into Richard's desk chair. Numbly she noticed that the desk and chair alone seemed untouched by the destruction. She couldn't even make out a speck of dust on the wood. The fan whirred on beside her.

"Maybe boys stick together," she muttered a little deliriously. "This shadow-child certainly seems to like you better than me, Richard."

She had no idea how long she sat there before finally pushing herself up and retrieving a broom and dustpan from the linen closet. She didn't bother turning on the lights in the rest of the house yet. There didn't seem to be any refuge in light, anyway. Day or night, light or bright, the shadow-boy did as it pleased.

She didn't allow herself to think about what she would do next. About recrafting her World Tree pots, or any pots. About how she would survive, practically, if this demon were intent on robbing her of every means of support. She focused on the sound of the broom bristles against the hardwood floor, the rattle of broken ceramic falling into the bin, the call of the night birds outside the window. She felt the exhaustion unwinding itself in long ribbons down her legs. She smelled sage and pine and dry earth.

When she was done sweeping, she grabbed a mop and filled a bucket with Pine-Sol and hot water. She scrubbed the floor till not a speck of dust clung to the boards. The odor stung her nose, weirdly intrusive in this remote place. Maybe intrusive was good. Maybe shadow-children didn't like Pine-Sol. She giggled weepily.

She found herself reluctant to stop cleaning, no matter how tired she was. Delaying tactic or coping mechanism, what was the difference, really? Her hands ached awfully, her joints wooden with swollen pain, but she ignored the sensations. Stubbornly she worked her way through the rest of the house till the floors shone like glass, turning on the lights in each room as she went till the place was ablaze.

She was basically an electricity camel, she told herself, at least until she needed to use her kiln. And God only knew when that would be. So she might as well use her power now. The sun would come up again tomorrow. Wouldn't it?

Eventually, though, she ran out of things to clean. Even the windowsills and baseboards were free of cobwebs and the fine brown dirt of the desert which blanketed everything. She ate standing at the kitchen sink, chewing without tasting a peanut butter sandwich as she stared blindly at the window. All she could see was her own bleak reflection. When the mouthless face of the shadow-boy materialized over her shoulder, she didn't even flinch. The white flames of its eyes seemed banked.

She didn't turn. She finished chewing the bite in her mouth and swallowed. "Feeling sheepish, are you? You aren't doing either of us any favors, you know."

The boy didn't move, but the cat-like tilt of its head made Hesper think it was listening to her, curiously.

"I'm not going to leave," she said flatly. "I'm not even sure that's what you want. Wouldn't you be lonely if no-one was here?"

It withdrew, ever so slightly.

"Although you're tormenting Leon Oberman, too, aren't you? Or what remains of him, whatever that is. A ghost or maybe just a powerful memory imprinted in this place by his grief, I don't know. I'm not much of an expert on the afterlife. But you seem to be quite enjoying making me miserable, so I don't imagine Leon alone is satisfying enough for you."

Its eyes grew hotter, and it seemed to strain against the darkness where a mouth should be. Hesper shuddered and glanced away.

"I'm suggesting we find a different means of interacting with each other besides you ruining everything good in my life and me running away from you. Something to think about."

Giving breath to the words drained her. She hadn't known she could feel even more exhausted. She turned her back to the window and sagged against the counter. The room appeared empty, but she knew better. At least she didn't seem to have taunted it into escalating. She looked at the recliner, all by itself in a pool of artificial light.

"I'm going to bed," she announced to anyone who was listening. "I'd like to actually get some sleep tonight, if you don't mind. I'll leave you alone if you leave me alone."

Tired, she showered, rinsing off the sweat and clay and residue of cleaning chemicals. She didn't turn out the light when she crawled into bed. The whole house was alight, and she intended to leave it that way. Richard sat on the bed with his back against the cornered walls, his arms open. She sighed deeply as she relaxed into his embrace, clutching at his fingers with her own unresponsive little nubs. All the aches and tension in her body unwound. The uncertainty of tomorrow remained there—tomorrow, though, was out of reach, unable to touch her in the fast today of Richard's arms.

"Quite the fight out there," he murmured against her hair.

"Yes." Hesper closed her eyes and tucked her head in the hollow of his breastbone.

"Eventually you're going to have to either defeat that thing or let it win, you know."

"I know? I don't know anything. I don't even know who—or what—that is."

"Of course you do." Richard tightened his grip. "Give it time, Hesper." Her name on his tongue warmed her heart. "But not too much time. That's no child, and it won't make friends."

"Mmm. Yes, sir."

"Do you want me to read to you?"

"Please."

She felt him rummaging under her pillow for her copy of Andrew Lang's *Red Book of Fairytales*. She had the whole series, but the grey and red were her favorites.

CHAPTER FIFTEEN

"Get up!" Richard was shoving her out of the bed. "Somebody's at the door."

"What? Who?"

"How would I know? But you should probably put some clothes on before you go. I'll be around."

"Sure, you will," Hesper grumbled, her fuzzy mind trying to think who it could be as she scrambled into a tank top and some overall shorts. She ran down the hallway, scraping a hand uselessly through her tangled hair. She squinted against the sunlight streaming into the house as she pulled the heavy wooden door open.

"Matilde!" she exclaimed, rational thought returning with something of a thud in her brain. "Matilde, I'm so sorry. I have no idea what time it is. I had kind of a late night, and I must have slept in. But come in, please."

The older woman was neat as a pin stabbed through a butterfly on a museum display, her iron-grey hair seemingly impervious to the desert breeze and her makeup impeccable. Her trim skirted suit managed to look both stylish and gypsy-inspired at the same time, the perfect balance for a gallery owner to strike. Hesper battened down a wave of envy, but Matilde smiled so warmly her jealousy vanished.

"No troubles. I think it's only about ten-thirty. I should have called first. It takes time to get settled into new patterns after a move. And I've been working in this business long enough to know that regular hours for an artist can be wildly different from regular hours for a shopkeeper. You don't owe me any explanations."

"How about some coffee instead of excuses, then?"

"Coffee is always lovely." Matilde followed Hesper the few steps into the kitchen, looking around curiously. "Do you have more furniture on the way? Or do you plan to purchase pieces here? I've always thought it's nice to start fresh with a move. Furniture bought for one house simply doesn't fit in another, most of the time."

Hesper's gaze followed Matilde's, across the empty expanse of the living room to the lone chair and TV tray with her laptop set on it. Licorice sticks, but it did look bare, didn't it? Furniture had been the last thing on her mind since she arrived. Her needs were fairly spartan, anyway.

"I guess I really haven't thought about it. None coming, though. My main priority was my kiln and my wheels and my equipment. Even this table came with the house."

Matilde's dark-complexioned skin flushed slightly, as if she were embarrassed by her question. "Of course. You have more important things on your mind."

"Cream? Sugar? I have some almond syrup and whipped cream, too, if you like."

"Oh, actually just a dash of that almond syrup sounds delicious, if you don't mind."

Hesper stirred some of the sugary concoction into both mugs and handed one to Matilde before topping her own off with whipped cream and cinnamon. She needed to come up to full power in a hurry.

Matilde took a couple of polite sips before her impatience clearly overcame her propriety.

"So, do you mind showing me Leon's paintings? I admit, I've been absolutely dying with anticipation since we spoke."

"I think you're definitely going to be surprised."

Hesper opened the cabinet door nearest Matilde. The woman gasped and jerked back, nearly dropping her mug.

Andy Oberman laughed out at her, joy cascading around his face in images at once familiar and indecipherable. Matilde placed her coffee on the table with trembling hands and stepped nearer to the painting, her fingers settling on the edge with utmost care.

"Why?" she whispered. "Why did he lock you away in there?"

One by one, Hesper opened every cabinet door in the kitchen. Matilde's eyes widened.

"Oh, Leon."

"And this isn't all. There's two more, in the closet and the bathroom cabinet. Thirteen in all."

Matilde lowered herself onto the bench seat, her back to the table, her gaze traveling over the many reincarnations of Andy Oberman. After a few moments, Hesper realized the

166

other woman's cheeks were wet with tears. But when Matilde spoke, her voice was clear.

"You must realize you have a fortune on your hands here."

"It's becoming evident," Hesper said, her tone dry.

"This would make an absolutely fabulous exhibition. The entire art world would be staggered. Each piece on its own is powerful, of course, but as a collection? I've never seen anything like it."

"A testament to love," Hesper said softly.

"Love? Is that what you see?"

"Don't you?"

Matilde slowly shook her head. "Don't mistake me. Leon loved his son dearly. I saw them together once, you know."

"I thought his son's death was the reason he moved out here?"

"Yes, but there was a reason he chose this place as a retreat. My gallery hosted an exhibition for Leon a couple of years before his son died, when his career was first beginning to really take off. He brought Andy with him. The two of them went everywhere together, I gathered. Andy was such a little thing then, maybe six or seven, and so sweet."

She paused, lost in recollection for a moment.

"I understood when Leon chose the Four Corners as his retreat from the world. The desert feels like a safe place after the city. But the truth is, the desert can be a dangerous locus for the grieving. This earth is full of spirits already. Those who come here broken apart by some trauma often find that those broken pieces take on a life of their own. They can be hurtful. Treacherous."

Hesper wondered if she should tell Matilde about her visions of Leon and the visits of the shadow-child. The gallery owner seemed like someone who would understand. Maybe even someone who could help. Still, she hesitated, her reluctance a mystery even to herself.

"So, you think the paintings represent some dark force?"

Matilde shrugged, a gesture meaning nothing and everything at once. "Maybe it's not so simple as that. I don't believe that locking away images of your dead child behind doors is love talking, though. Regret, maybe. Remorse. Guilt. Obsession, even. But love doesn't lock away."

"Do you know how Andy died?"

Matilde nodded soberly. "Complications of pneumonia. The little fellow was forever getting sick, and one day he was out in a cold rain at the bus stop. Not for long, I think. But long enough."

Images of the street of memories bound in the mirror frame flashed through Hesper's mind. "Leon forgot to pick him up. He was on a date."

Matilde shot her a sharp look, and her expression darkened. "I didn't think you knew much of anything about Leon Oberman or what happened. How do you know that?"

"I—uh—I think maybe the realtor said something after I found the paintings hidden behind the shelf paper she'd pasted up."

Suspicion deepened the lines between Matilde's brows. "Huh. I'm surprised she'd know that much. Leon was wrong to blame himself. He was only maybe five minutes late. And even that wouldn't have been so bad if Andy's umbrella hadn't gotten whipped inside out by the wind. Poor kid was soaked through when Leon drove up. But it was a few minutes late, one time in the boy's life. None of us can order fortune, however much we try to barter with time for second chances. For all Leon knew, Andy was already sick when he sent him to school that day and the symptoms just hadn't shown up yet."

"I'm surprised Leon even put him on a bus, as close as they seemed to be."

"Oh, that was all Andy. He wanted to be like the other kids, you know? To fit in. And Leon wanted that for him, too. So, he drove Andy back and forth to the bus stop nearest their apartment every day. Andy wanted to be ordinary. And sadly, ordinary kids are very mortal. But Leon couldn't accept that."

Hesper understood, much better than she wanted to.

Matilde spent the next hour poring over the paintings. Hesper realized after a while it was as much about authenticating them as understanding them. She hadn't even thought about the likelihood of art fraud around these pieces, but especially given the sad history of the estate, she supposed it was too probable to ignore. It would be quite clever—and no doubt lucrative—for a con artist to combine imitations of Leon Oberman's style with representations of his high-drama-value grief.

What sons of cinnamon sticks people were, Hesper reflected.

"These are definitely Leon Oberman originals," Matilde finally announced. "I would have to consult with some other people before I could tell you for sure, but I'm guessing this is at least a few hundred thousand dollars' worth of paintings. Until I can get back to you, Hesper, you should really be very careful."

"Careful?" That's not what Hesper was expecting to hear.

"New Mexico has always been a badlands, and that hasn't changed. In fact, in addition to the run-of-the-mill outlaws and fugitives who've always refuged here, the art and archaeology scene has brought its own brand of bandits. I'll be as discreet as I can making inquiries—I have people I trust. But you shouldn't say anything to anyone. Although I'd be very surprised if that real estate agent has kept her mouth shut. And call your homeowner's insurance. This place just got way, way more valuable."

Hesper's head spun. She tried to seize on a single detail.

"I don't think Gloria—the realtor—told anyone. She's

the one who papered over them. She thought they were creepy and would bring down the value."

Matilde snorted. "I have zero confidence in a realtor's ability to keep their mouths shut about anything, let alone something they consider creepy. Thank God she didn't throw the doors out altogether and replace them before she put the house on the market."

The gallery owner downed the dregs of her third cup of coffee. "Now. Since I'm here, anyway, why don't you show me some of your own pieces? That is why you came by the gallery initially, after all."

Hesper grimaced. "Oh. Yes. I'd actually forgotten. There was a—mishap—in my studio last night. Some pieces got broken."

Matilde frowned. "Well, show me what you have, then. I can at least get a sense of your style, even if it isn't enough for a show right now."

"Yeah, I should have said all my pieces got broken."

The suspicion that had died away from Matilde's expression came roaring back. "All your pieces?"

Hesper nodded, her chest tight.

"What the hell happened?"

"I left the window open," Hesper said. "A strong wind must have knocked everything off the shelves."

"Show me your studio," Matilde demanded flatly.

Hesper led the way down the hall, relieved to see the

door to the studio still stood open. Hopefully the shadow-child wouldn't make an appearance with Matilde here and wreak any new devastation. Not that there was much left to destroy.

"Right here."

Matilde stood in the middle of the room and did a slow pivot. Hesper wondered if the other woman saw more than what met the eye: empty shelves, full buckets of clay, sparkling clean floors, an empty wheel. Richard's desk under the window. The little fan humming meekly along. Hesper hoped the other woman didn't suspect her of being some moneyed hobbyist who'd just gone out and bought her supplies and who simply hadn't produced anything yet.

That was silly, Hesper told herself. Matilde had surely checked Hesper Dunn out online before driving all the way out here, had seen her gallery shows going back years in studios all over the Midwest and East Coast.

Matilde walked over to the shelves, fingered Hesper's tools that lay there in a neat line. "I don't know what you're playing at, but no wind blew anything off these shelves. Definitely didn't blow any heavy-ass pottery off. Don't get too caught up in the temperamental artist schtick. It gets old when it interferes with deadlines and delivery dates. And I don't work with people I can't trust."

Whew. The gallery owner was assuming Hesper had broken all her own pots in a fit of pique or something. Not that Hesper believed her protestations about only working with trustworthy artists for a minute. No way did Matilde intend to walk away from this Leon Oberman collection. Of that Hesper had no doubt.

But she only nodded.

Matilde wiped her perfectly clean hands down the front of her skirt. "All right, then. I'll get back to you with a rough estimate for all thirteen pieces as a collection. Once I get them to the gallery, we'll have an expert come in and price each one individually as well. But I think we should agree to hold out for some time to try and sell it as a series. I already know a few museums I can contact who might want it as part of their permanent collection."

Oh, Matilde moved fast when she was motivated.

"Wait up," Hesper said. "I don't want to sell the one in the mirror frame in the bathroom at all."

Matilde spun slowly back to face Hesper, her eyes narrowed. "I'd really like to have the complete collection. And I think we both know that one is the seminal piece."

Hesper shook her head. "No."

"Are you wanting to sell it on its own, as a standalone?"

"I'm not selling it at all. It belongs in this house. It shouldn't go anywhere."

Matilde tilted her head. "You seem very emotionally invested, considering you only recently learned who Leon was."

Hesper had never been inclined to explain herself to others. "I'm not selling it. It stays with the house."

Slowly, Matilde nodded. "All right. Will you at least let me know first if you change your mind?"

"Sure." That was an easy promise to make. Hesper wasn't going to change her mind.

"Well, thank you for the coffee. I'll be in touch when I have more solid information for you, and we'll schedule a time for an evaluator to come out. I would like to get these doors down and stored safely as soon as possible. It would be tragic to have one damaged by a falling plate or a splash of grease. I don't know what Leon was thinking, honestly. These paintings were bound to get fouled up in a kitchen, of all places."

Hesper saw the other woman out. She stood there in the warm light long after Matilde's car had vanished in a cloud of dust. Hesper thought maybe she understood why Leon had chosen that placement for his son's images. Besides the emotional impact of having the child locked away on the other side of every door he could find, that is. As a father, surely, he wanted his son's presence to be ordinary rather than hallowed, incidental rather than conserved. Hesper imagined he'd looked forward to the day when the paintings grew gently battered and dinged and stained with the oil of his fingers. It was as close as he would ever get, now, to watching his son change and age over time. The casual wear of commonplace contact would have given Andy's presence an aspect of companionship instead of the stately regard of a well-guarded prize. A father didn't want his son to be a masterpiece. He just wanted him to be there.

Hesper understood that. Somewhere still taped up in a box sat a gleaming maple urn full of ashes. She didn't want to give those remains a place of honor. She didn't want to construct some sort of shrine in her home. She didn't want to dust and polish the wood, to keep cold and clean its brass engraving. She didn't want all that was left to be sacred and antiseptic.

She shuddered away the thought, closing the front door. She still had two tapestries to decipher. Maybe once she'd learned from them what she could, she'd call Ginny and calm her fears. Ginny would appreciate that.

Sunlight was falling across the fifth tapestry panel. *Smell.* It struck Hesper as the most idyllic of the tapestries. The Lion and the Unicorn both looked on contentedly as the Lady wove flower chains from a basket of blossoms held by her lady-in-waiting. Serenity reigned. The only bit of whimsy was in the little monkey who'd stolen a flower for himself and had his face buried in its sweet petals.

Hesper almost imagined she drew that heavy, honeyed air into her own lungs. Intoxicating, stultifying. Masking. Lying.

Discomfort intruded in what should have been peace. In

the Middle Ages, fragrance was used to cover up the rotten aromas of reality. Even the nobility of that age would have been surrounded by the odors of unwashed bodies, old sweat, sewage in the streets and in the chamber pots, rancid meat, milling livestock. Perfumes and oils and herbs plastered a crumbling beauty over all that was putrefying and oozing.

The Lady's titled position was as much a farce as a daisy-chain around the neck of a donkey. It wasn't enough for her to walk among the rows of blooming stalks and bushes and trees and inhale their ambrosial oxygen. No, the Lady must pluck and bend them into the shape of dissemblage for those beyond the reach of their fragrance. This panel was all about distortion and fraud, fakery and mendacity.

Maybe what looked like serenity was actually brainwashed resignation, Hesper thought. The very perfection of the scene jangled. Like watching a Stepford wife mix up a batch of brownies. How sad, to be surrounded by beauty and find one's task had been set to tear it apart, to manipulate it into crude necklaces that could only wither and brown. Or maybe the Lady was more than willing to play the part as long as it allowed her to plot an escape. Maybe she even delighted in the dull credulity, the willingness of the senses to be seduced, that would facilitate her getaway.

"Blegh."

Hesper left the tapestries and walked outside to check on

her clay. She wasn't sure how to proceed. She had a little time, but Marcy expected that World Tree collection sooner than later. Pottery wasn't exactly a rush job. And while Hesper still held the presences of the four directions vividly in her mind's eye, recreating them would nonetheless be a major undertaking. And there was no reason to believe that shadow-child wouldn't immediately destroy them again. It wasn't like she could sleep with them under her pillow.

Getting rid of those cabinet doors had to have some sort of impact on the hauntings here. Whether that would help, Hesper had no idea. She had to do something.

The scents of pine needles, sun-warmed sage, and dry earth enveloped Hesper. The world smelled clean and real and powerful, full of possibility. She wouldn't trade this for any high-dollar perfume or melting oil or wilting petals.

Walking to the tree where the clay hung in sheets from a low limb, she hefted its weight in her hands. Satisfaction rumbled through her. This must be how the gods feel, she thought, when they carry a world in their palms. She dragged the ladder over and untied the bundle from its limb. The trip back down the ladder was more than a little precarious, but she managed.

She wheelbarrowed the bundle over to the courtyard. Funny how simple tasks like this made her feel so capable. That shadow-child had no idea who it was dealing with.

She dumped the wheelbarrow over onto the flagstones,

unwinding the mound of clay from the sheets. Using her fists and the heels of her hands, she pounded out the clay where it could finish drying completely in the sun. She really had no idea what she was doing, but she enjoyed it anyway. There was something so sensual, so fundamental, about the process. And if it took her any number of failures to get the ratios and the temperatures correct so that the pots didn't shatter in the kiln, that was all right. She'd never been afraid of being wrong.

Somewhere she'd read some potters mixed fine rocks in with their clay to help it hold itself together. She could look for some native gravel while she was out on her walks too. Maybe she'd end up resorting to a mix of wild clay and her catalogue clays, but she wanted to attempt some fully feral pots first.

She grinned at the thought.

CHAPTER SIXTEEN

Hesper washed up in the bathroom. She liked to watch the swirl of grey slurry disappearing down the sink drain. It was like another claiming of her territory. She raised her head and stared into the reflection of her own eyes. Or were those Leon's eyes, darker and wider than her own, looking back at her?

"You understand, don't you?" Hesper murmured. "I can share this space with you forever. But that other creature—it's going to destroy the both of us if I don't drive it out."

The sadness that always typified Leon's gaze deepened, and he shook his head. Hesper didn't know if he actually disagreed with her, or if he doubted her ability to succeed.

"No matter," she said. "I'll believe enough for the both of us."

She couldn't have explained exactly when or how she'd come to identify so strongly with Leon Oberman, or why she was so certain that his intentions toward her weren't malevolent. But somehow she'd decided he needed her help, that he was as much at the mercy of the shadow-child as she was. Maybe more so, since the two of them must be on the same side of the shade. Right? Although, the shadow-child didn't seem to have any difficulty crossing into the temporal plane when it wanted to wreak some destruction.

That meant its threat to her wasn't theoretical or purely

psychological. If it could smash her pots, it could smash her too.

And who knew what it might do to Richard? That didn't bear considering. No, she had to handle this situation, sooner than later.

She dried her arms and headed to the studio to check on her husband. He was working away at his desk, as she expected, sunlight gleaming on his bent head. Her heart swelled as he turned and stood to greet her, wrapping her up in his arms without hesitation.

"That gallery lady stayed a long time," he observed.

She nodded against his chest. "I hope we didn't bother you too much. She spent quite a while looking at the cabinet paintings. And then I laid out my wild clay to dry before I came back here."

"Didn't bother me at all." He brushed her hair off her forehead. "You know I don't mind company."

"I think I'll go ahead and remove the cabinet doors," she told him. "Matilde is going to send someone out to take a closer look and then we'll be moving them to her gallery for a major exhibition sometime soon. She pointed out they might get damaged, being constantly used, and she's right."

"Are you sure that's a good idea? It seems a little...provocative."

"I'm okay with provocative."

"Has that worked well so far?" Richard gestured to her

empty shelves, his blue eyes darkening from clear sky to stormy sea with worry.

"I'm certainly not going to concede defeat. Whatever else is here with us, it doesn't get to decide what we do or how we live. If it wants a fight, I'll give it a real battle. And it isn't right for Leon's work to be locked away here. The world should see what he created."

"Is that what he wanted?"

"No, I don't think it was. But artists are wrong about their own work all the time. We only get to own the process. Everything that comes after—that belongs to the world, not to us."

"That's very generous." Richard's voice was dry, and she knew why. However much she might believe what she was saying, the philosophy was easier to adopt with regard to anyone's work but her own. She'd been known to say more than a few unkind words herself about the perspective of reviewers on her exhibitions. Emotional venting, though, wasn't the same as principled thought, and she did champion the independence of the viewer's experience, even if she didn't always like it.

So, now, she shrugged. "Not really. No work of art is complete except in the heart of each person who experiences it. That's not generous—it's just reality. And just like my intent doesn't need their validation, I don't have to validate their interpretation."

Richard chuckled. "Yeah, I know, you don't read write-ups or reviews of your shows."

"I don't need to. I did what I had to do. What anyone else thinks of that is beside the point. For me. For them, it is the point, obviously."

"Obviously. So, you're going to put Leon Oberman's work on exhibition whether that's what he wanted or not?"

"Yes." She spoke without apology. "Every artist knows that's a risk they take. Every writer who leaves a draft unburned or painter who leaves a sketchbook lying on a shelf knows what might become of it if the next moment is their last. And since artists rarely think about anything besides love and death, protests to the contrary are pathetically unconvincing."

"I love how you assume all artists feel just like you."

"What can I say? I don't think I'm all that unique. Humility. My signal trait." She snickered.

"And what happens to the paintings after the exhibit closes?"

"We're going to try to sell them to a museum, so they can keep traveling and stay on display, either as a permanent exhibition or by going from one museum to another. I'm sure Matilde would love to keep them for her own gallery, but there's no way she has the capital for that."

Richard whistled. "That has to mean a serious chunk of change."

"We definitely won't have a mortgage anymore."

"Are you sure you have the—what's it called?—is it provenance?—for that? I mean, I'd think Leon Oberman had some heirs or something that would want to lay claim to his work."

Hesper shrugged. "Maybe? But if he does, they didn't bother to claim the house and the debts he'd incurred by his death. That's why the bank ended up seizing the place. I don't get the impression he was exactly a financial wizard, even though his work was commanding high dollar values by the time of his death. All his son's educational and medical costs came out of pocket. There's no benefits package to being an artist, as you know. So, since anyone who might be out there who'd want to claim a connection with him allowed the house to be sold, with all its furnishings, that means the paintings are mine. I think."

"Wow."

"I know, right? But them's the breaks."

Hesper moved out of his embrace, running her hands restlessly over her empty shelves. "At any rate, my priority now is to reclaim this space for us."

"Us?"

She turned on him with something like fury. "*Us.*"

He raised his hands in surrender. "All right, all right. Us."

"And whatever that shadow-child is, I think maybe it feeds off something in those paintings. If I can send them away, I'll starve it out."

"You still insist you don't know what it is, huh?"

"I wish you wouldn't talk in riddles, Richard. Just say what you're thinking."

His hands dropped on her shoulders, and he pressed a kiss to her forehead before whispering, "You won't let me."

She choked on an unexpected sob. "I need to find the screwdriver."

She spun and left him, her eyes blinded with tears she frantically blinked away.

The house was oddly quiet as she worked, unscrewing each cabinet door from its hinges. Those blankets she'd bought from the moving company were turning out to come in very handy, indeed. She stacked the painted doors with folds of the blankets between them. She wished she had somewhere outside the house she could store them, but the only other building on the property besides that rickety shed was the outhouse. And while that technically had enough room, it definitely wasn't an acceptable space for storing paintings. So, she created a pillar of doors and blankets in the corner of the living room.

She'd expected some pushback, some resistance, but the afternoon was still and silent as she worked. Only the wheezing effort of the fans even kept the air moving. Robbed of its doors, the kitchen looked oddly vulnerable and ashamed when she was done.

"I'll find you some clothes," she promised the stripped cabinets. "Maybe the Habitat for Humanity store will have some spare cabinet doors. A little variety might be fun, anyway. Fanciful. I could paint each one a different color. Get a different pull for each knob. Crystal and brass and wood. Conformity is for plebs, after all."

Surely Santa Fe had a ReStore. If not, there had to be a salvage or something where she could find random cabinet doors. Hopefully they came in generally standard sizes. She wasn't exactly a handywoman. In the meantime, she'd have to get used to the gaping kitchen shelves. Luckily, they weren't exactly overflowing with their contents. And she didn't need to worry about earthquakes in the desert. Did she?

She leaned wearily on the island. Food, she thought..

Thirty minutes later, she took a pot of habanero-and-bacon macaroni-and-cheese and a soda out onto the courtyard to eat.

"Licorice sticks," she muttered through gritted teeth at the scene that met her view.

All her clay that ought to have been nearly dry by now was drenched through. It looked like someone had dumped a bucket of water over it all. Or—her eyes narrowed as she glared around the seemingly empty courtyard—stood over it and peed on the clay.

Stubbornly she carried her dinner over to the stone table

and metal chair that had come with the place. She banged the hot pot down and scraped her chair forward.

"What a delicious supper," she said loudly. "It will be lovely to watch the sunset while I eat. A perfect night."

Logically, she knew the shadow-boy hadn't peed on her clay. Shadow-boys didn't have pee, right? No guts, no bladder. But then, how had he manipulated water in any form? Regardless of how he'd managed it, he was clearly determined to ruin her efforts.

The gooey hot cheese and pasta momentarily distracted her from ire. No gourmet chef, but she had mastered a few comfort foods all the same.

Hesper stretched her legs out and squinted against the flaming colors unraveling across the evening skies like dropped skeins of brilliant wool. She made short work of her supper, eating half the pot before darkness had fallen. And now she had food for tomorrow. She had no doubt the house was going to protest her incursions on its structure tonight.

She shivered, suddenly aware the heat had gone out of the thin desert air. Her bluster and bravado dissipated with the light. She wasn't sure which was worse, sitting in the courtyard waiting for the shadows to come out of the trees and join her, or stepping back inside the malevolence lurking in the house.

Richard, though. Richard was inside, waiting for her.

Casting a last look of scorn at the puddled clay, she

grabbed her saucepan and empty soda can and headed inside. She tried not to regret taking the cabinet doors down as she walked into the kitchen to wash out her pan. Somehow, she felt as exposed as the dishes and glasses and canned goods standing there. Defenseless.

She flipped on all the lights in the house, ignoring Richard's quiet laughter when she passed the studio.

"Are you still working?" she asked.

He rolled his chair around and quirked his brows over his glasses at her. "Seems to be what I do most days. Always preparing, never arriving."

Regret tightened her jaw. "You should relax. Just enjoy yourself. Be here."

His smile was sad. "Of course."

"I'm going to shower. Maybe turn in early tonight."

"Sounds good, babe. I'll meet you in bed."

At least the shower was nice and hot. She'd thought she might want to take cold showers, living in the desert, but having sweat and dust stuck to her skin all day only made her want a lovely steam all the more. She tried not to psych herself out with horror movie scenarios about hands on the other side of the shower curtain or some evil black mist rising out of the drain, but she still found herself winding tighter and tighter with anxiety. She rushed through a shampoo and shave, pulling back the plastic curtain and sighing with relief to see she was still the only person in the small room.

She flipped her hair upside down and toweled vigorously before winding the bright red cloth around her head and straightening. She'd thought she was prepared for anything, but she couldn't help shrieking when she saw the shattered mirror over the sink.

Broken edges cobwebbed away from an impact crater in the center of the mirror, looking for all the world as if someone had punched it. A single shard was missing. With a trembling finger, Hesper traced the long, jagged, narrow wood where it had been.

"It's your fault," a deep voice rasped. Leon Oberman was standing in the broken mirror, his haunted eyes shining with tears. He was talking to himself, Hesper realized. There, clutched in his hand, on the other side of the mirror, was the missing piece.

"No! Leon, don't do it. It wasn't your fault. It was just an accident."

"It's your fault. You don't deserve to be here. He's the one who should be here, not you."

Was that Leon's voice, or her own? Hesper covered her ears with her hands. Leon's splintered face morphed into Richard's, canted at that horrible, horrible angle. His open eyes staring and bloodshot and already growing opaque. Blood, blood, everywhere.

She curled over, clutching her stomach. Warm, red liquid

dripped onto the tile floor. Was it hers? Or Leon's? Or Richard's? Was it there at all?

"There's no such thing as an accident. You wanted this."

She shook her head, fighting sobs. "No. No. We would have worked through things. We *have* worked through things. I love Richard. He loves me. Nothing else matters."

A hollow laugh, more grief than amusement, bounced around the bathroom walls. "I was tired. So tired. I stole one hour for myself, and that one hour ended up being Andy's whole life. You can't lie to me. I won't lie to myself."

"It was a mistake!" Hesper sank back on her heels, leaning wearily against the wall. She rubbed her fingers idly. The blood, it seemed, was her own, though she wasn't sure how she'd cut herself. Richard's ghastly apparition was gone, and only Leon remained, more presence than incarnation.

"You have to forgive yourself."

A crash sounded from the kitchen. Hesper started to her feet, terror rocketing through her as she clutched her blood-soaked towel closer.

Another crash. Then another.

She ran down the hallway. The shadow-boy crouched on the kitchen counter like a praying mantis, its eye sockets burning. She could hear that wretched song, though the creature still had no mouth.

"You are my SUNSHINE..."

Crash.

"...*my* only SUNSHINE!"

Crash.

The shadow-boy raised plate after plate over his head and hurled them onto the floor as it punctuated its song. Next came the glasses. The canned goods, rolling and dented. Hesper retreated across the living room, out of reach of glass and ceramic shrapnel. The shadow-boy hopped from one counter to another. She didn't need to see a facial expression to know maniacal glee fueled its destruction.

"Stop," she whispered helplessly. "What do you want? Please, please stop."

There was no way it could hear her over the sounds of shattering kitchenware and its own merry singing. Maybe she was talking to herself.

Suddenly it stopped, its arm upraised and clutching a can of tomatoes. Hesper followed its arrested gaze. Leon Oberman stood in the hallway opening, his face sober and despairing, his arms open. The shadow-boy clambered over the sink, dropping the can heedlessly on the floor, and climbed into the ghost's embrace. Leon gripped the demon close, burying his face in what would have been a child's hair. He cast a single remorseful glance at Hesper before disappearing.

She collapsed into her recliner, knees shaking so hard she didn't know if she'd ever be able to stand again. What had just happened? Had Leon Oberman come to save her from the wild chaos of the creature he had to know was no son of his? And here she had been thinking he was the one who needed her help.

What was she missing? Were Leon and the shadow-child enemies or allies? She didn't fear the dead artist. All she sensed from him was sadness, not malevolence. If anything, he seemed to be trying to bridge a gap, to make a connection with her. As if he recognized something of himself in her. As she recognized herself in him.

For her part, she wished she could find a way to untether him from this place. Not because she minded his company. She suspected she would always hear echoes of his voice in the wind here, always find his footprints in the dust. Some spirits were too strong not to leave a mark. But she was certain Leon Oberman was trapped here. However desperate and misguided his decision to take his own life, it ought to have at least freed him from this plane so far from his beloved son. Instead, he had somehow bound himself inescapably here. There had to be a way to help him. A way to unknot the cord.

But the shadow-child...Hesper couldn't help believing it had something to do with Leon's imprisonment here. It had no intention of letting him go. She wasn't even sure if it was trying to drive her away or just drive her mad. Maybe it wanted to keep her, too. But why?

Was it some sort of spirit vampire, drawing its energy

and animus from others? Pondering the existence of such a creature should qualify her for the loony bin but the shadow-boy was as unquestionably real as the crickets singing outside her door or the scarlet chili peppers swinging on their hook. But how to starve the thing? So far, everything she did only antagonized and strengthened it. She hoped it wasn't actually increasing in corporality. It was no less dangerous than any human assailant. In fact, she was sure it was much *more* dangerous.

Why would Leon embrace the thing? Leon Oberman had to know exactly what the imp really was. Richard insisted that she knew, too. But that was nonsense. She'd never encountered anything like it before in her life. She wasn't prone to flights of imagination or superstition. These last few months had been an aberration. So why had Richard suggested she'd have some secret knowledge of mouthless shadow-children with flaming eyes?

Despair, dark and liquid and languid, washed over her in heavy, undulating waves.

CHAPTER SEVENTEEN

Again? Seriously?

Her pills formed a little ring, a parade of white tablets, around the bathroom sink. "Not very subtle, Richard," she grumbled. He knew what the consequences would be if she took those mastodon-munchers. She had no intention of going there. She brushed her teeth and hair, moving gingerly to avoid so much as touching one of the tablets. "Two can play at this game."

She'd lost track of the days. Lost track of her own objectives. Everything she attempted turned to ash in her hands. She'd abandoned the effort to harvest her own clay. Not permanently, just until she could rid her home of its nasty infection. But even when she attempted to work the clay she'd brought with her, she was foiled. It didn't matter whether she used her electric wheel in the studio or the foot-powered wheel in the courtyard. No sooner had she begun to find the shape waiting in the cool, slippy clay, the shadow-boy would creep up behind her, seize her hands in a fierce grasp, and smash and pound the nascent pot to sludge.

Her oasis was no longer an idyll. She didn't bother trying to tidy up. Dried clay lay in heaps and streaks on the flagstones outside and on the hardwood floor in front of Richard's desk. Ceramic dust, shattered glass, and shards of plates and bowls littered the kitchen floor and the dining room table. When she got hungry, she scooped a dented can off the floor and ate right out of it. Or retrieved a slice of bread from the smashed loaf still on the counter. The coffee maker was broken, too, so no coffee for her. She'd polished off the Fireball last night? The night before?

Richard was at a loss. He still read to her at night, still held her till she fell asleep. But she knew he was unhappy with her. It wasn't just her refusal to take her medication. Somehow, he held her responsible for what was happening with the shadow-boy.

"You have to stop this," he told her softly, his long fingers brushing her hair.

"I want to. I'm trying to. But nothing is working."

"You aren't trying."

"Everything I do makes it worse."

"Stop pretending you don't know what's happening."

"I *don't*. I never even heard of Leon Oberman before we moved here. And I've certainly never encountered anything remotely like that awful monster. Why on earth wouldn't I get rid of it if I could? All I want is for it to leave us alone."

"That's not what you want."

Tears welled unexpectedly. "You can't hold that against me."

"Of course I can. You have one responsibility, Hesper. To live. And you're refusing."

Leon Oberman's words echoed in her memory.

It's your fault. You don't deserve to be here. He's the one who should be here, not you.

"I'm trying." Her words unconvincing.

"You need to try harder. You need to banish that imp before it destroys you."

Hesper set her jaw, but she couldn't resist turning her head deeper into Richard's chest. She hated when he talked like this. It was as if at any moment he might stand up, walk away, and never come back. As if somehow she was supposed to live without him. Whatever else happened, she couldn't allow that.

She no longer went on desert walks. What was the point? The farthest she went was to the verge of her little stand of trees. She'd sit on the warm ground, barely out of reach of the gleaming sun, and watch bugs and lizards bustle about their chores. One day she even saw a roadrunner. A giggle escaped as she watched it dart over the ground, and the sound startled her. She didn't know the last time she laughed.

Soon enough she'd run out of groceries. She should drive into town for supplies, but starting the car seemed an enormity of its own. Actually driving the long road into town, braving the store, and driving home would be impossible. It took every ounce of energy she had to move from one room to another, from the courtyard to the shade of the trees. How could she manage that great heap of steel and glass and gasoline?

She was still showering at some sort of intervals, though she wasn't sure what they were. That meant she wasn't depressed, right? As long as she still brushed her hair and cleaned her body, there was nothing to worry about. When she tried to decipher what she was doing, exactly, her thoughts got muddy.

I need to outwait the shadow-boy, she told herself. That's what I'm doing. Persisting.

Weirdly enough, the shadow-boy hadn't taken advantage of her lethargy. The deeper she sank into doldrums, the quieter it grew. She wasn't sure how much lower she could go and still breathe, though.

Had this been part of what drove Leon Oberman to take his own life? She'd been assuming the shadow-boy hadn't appeared till after Leon's death, but she had no reason to think that now that she considered the matter. Maybe Leon had found the shadow-child here when he moved in. Maybe he'd brought the dark creature with him from the home he'd shared with his son.

That thought pricked at her consciousness like a thistle.

Why, or how, would Leon have brought the shadow-child with him? Hesper knew, down to her bones, it wasn't the ghost of his dead child. What other sort of spirit would attach itself so powerfully to him?

And to her.

They'd both suffered. Both tried, for a while, at least, to come back from tragedy. Could it be as simple as remorse?

No. Hesper shook her head. Remorse was a weak thing. An unworthy thing. She knew firsthand remorse lacked any power at all. Whatever fed the shadow-boy was strong, stronger than Leon had been, maybe stronger than her, too.

Hesper could feel that black seething hatred, even now. She could look around for it, but there was no point in that. She lost every battle she mounted with it. And lately, it seemed content to glut itself on her burgeoning misery. The bleaker and stranger her thoughts, the more sedate it became. Fat and docile and content.

Again and again her mind turned to the puzzle of Leon's death. She'd thought at first it was simple grief. He hadn't been able to bear up under the sadness and had tried to go home, to be with his son. But that didn't add up. Hesper was beginning to suspect the shadow-boy had been behind Leon's suicide. Whatever trick it had used to convince Leon to stab himself in the neck with that broken mirror, it had used to condemn Leon to haunt this place still, forever divided from his child.

Grimly, Hesper eyed the stack of paintings still wrapped carefully in their blankets. It struck her as downright bizarre the shadow-boy hadn't battered them into splinters yet. Come to think of it, about the only things in the house it hadn't destroyed were Ginny's tapestries and that stack of paintings.

Maybe there was something about the paintings, something the shadow-boy valued even more than she did. As for the tapestries, she suspected it hadn't gotten to them yet. There wasn't much it could do to them besides tear them off the wall, she supposed. They were too tightly woven for its fingers to unravel. She thought. She hoped.

She sighed. It'd get to them eventually.

But the paintings...there had been that one night it slammed the cabinet doors. So it wasn't ignoring or avoiding the paintings. Now, she couldn't even remember what it was she'd said before the smashing started. Her mental processes were lost in a permanent fog. And not some romantic windswept wisps, either. Pea soup. Sea fog. The stuff that stranded ships for days. Weeks.

What could the paintings signify to the shadow-boy?

Normally, Hesper was a big believer that every work of art was unique in the experience of each person who encountered it. But now she was stone-cold certain whatever the paintings meant to Leon were what they meant to the shadow-boy, and therein lay their value. Maybe even their power.

What was it Matilde had said about the paintings? Hesper had thought they were a testament to love persisting even beyond the closed door of death. But Matilde had thought they spoke to something much more sinister. Obsession. Guilt.

Like a flash, Hesper remembered what she'd said to Leon in the moment before the shadow-boy commenced his kitchen tantrum.

Forgive yourself.

The paintings didn't represent devotion, they represented condemnation. In every embodiment of his son, Leon had painted his own culpability. In painful and exacting strokes, he inventoried each aspect of what his son's death had stolen. Pensive, laughing, sad, confused, distracted, daydreaming, all the faces of Andy he'd never see again, on that side of the door he couldn't find a way through himself. Instead of memory, the paintings had stood in accusation. In denunciation.

Hesper pushed herself to her feet and shambled down the hall to the bathroom. Leaning on the sink but carefully avoiding the little promenade of pills, she peered into the broken mirror. Leon Oberman stared soberly back at her. Over his shoulder, she could see darkness misting and roiling, a sinister black cloud.

"I'm close," she told him. "I know I'm close. What were you thinking? What did you want to do?"

He vanished at the rumbling sound of a car engine outside.

"Licorice sticks," Hesper grumbled. It must be that

appraiser Matilde had scheduled. She'd called Hesper the day after her visit with a date and time, but details like that had ceased to have any meaning. It could have been a week ago or two days ago.

She had clothes on, anyway. And she'd brushed her hair sometime fairly recently, she thought. Not that she cared how some stranger judged her fashion sense. They could take her as she was, or they could leave.

She'd nearly reached the door when a familiar voice accompanying the knock stopped her in her tracks.

"Hesper? Hesper, it's Ginny. I know you're home. I can see your car out here."

Ginny? What was Ginny doing here?

Hesper opened the door. Sure enough, there was her sister-in-law. Hesper's heart seized. How had she forgotten how alike Ginny and Richard looked? They might have been fraternal twins. Ginny wore a floppy straw hat and a fiercely ugly muumuu whose only redeeming quality was its brilliant and terrifyingly complete palette of colors. But no swaths of hideous fabric could disguise the strong, unguarded beauty of her facial structure, her square jaw and those striking blue eyes.

Blue eyes just like Richard's.

Blue eyes just now sparking with worry and if Hesper wasn't mistaken, out-and-out horror. Hesper must not be maintaining that personal hygiene thing quite as well as she thought.

"What the ham sandwiches are you doing here?" tumbled out of her mouth before she could stop herself.

Ginny snorted and promptly teared up at the ridiculous obscenity. "Lord. I haven't heard that nonsense since—since you moved. And what do you think I'm doing here? You had to know I was coming. You haven't answered your phone in a week. No emails. No nothing. You could've been dead in a ditch. You don't get to drop out of life, Hesper. You belong to people. Now let me in. I'm tired and hot and I need to pee."

Hesper stepped back with alacrity. "Sure. Of course. Sorry. Come in. It's—ah—it's a bit of a mess." She waved her hands weakly. "There's been some—stuff—going on."

Ginny came to a hard stop about five feet into the house, her eyes going wide. She gave a low whistle and shook her head as she took in the scene: broken dishes and glasses and dust covering the floor, cans and boxes of food, some torn open and spilling across the counters, empty containers and bottles littered among it all.

"Bathroom?" was all she said, though.

Hesper gestured. "Down the hall. Second door on the right."

Ginny closed the door quietly behind her, though Hesper heard a decidedly not-elementary-school-ready ejaculation when Ginny no doubt saw the broken mirror. Was there still blood on the floor? Hesper couldn't remember. The toilet was functional, at least. And there was toilet paper. That had to count for something, right?

She perched on the edge of her recliner, rising hastily when she heard Ginny coming back. She'd have to clean off the table and the bench seats so there'd be more than one chair to sit on. For now, the rocker would have to do.

"Have a seat," she said, wanting to laugh out loud at the ridiculous civility. "I'll clean things up."

Who knew how that would go? Would the shadow-child come out to oppose her even with Ginny here? Would Ginny be able to see it?

Ginny eyed the recliner fiercely before settling into it, as if giving it a silent warning not to eject her. Hesper couldn't blame her for being suspicious. It certainly looked as if the house and she had been engaged in battle.

Hesper retrieved a broom and dustpan from the closet. At least there was almost nothing left to break. Although she'd be quite blue if the little imp took to the windows. They were open all the time, of course, but if the shadow-boy broke out the glass and shredded her screens, she'd have no defense against all the flying bugs and scorpions and spiders. And snakes, for that matter. The desert was much more hospitable to life than most people realized. It just wasn't usually furry and cuddly life.

Hesper wasn't normally one of those people who rushed to fill any pause with inanities, but Ginny had a gift for speaking silences. Hesper only held out a couple minutes before she gave in.

"It's not what it looks like. Actually, I have no idea what it looks like. But there's been something going on here. Something I can't explain. A presence. And it doesn't like me much."

Ginny leaned back into the chair like it was a throne, her hands curling over the arms as she pivoted to face Hesper directly. Her eyebrows quirked doubtfully. "A presence?"

"You know I told you about the artist who lived and died here before me." She scooped a pile of broken crockery into a trash bag.

"So, he's not particularly hospitable?"

"He's not the problem. Or, I guess he probably is part of it, but he's not hostile in any way. He's just very sad. But there's something else here. I call it a shadow-child."

"A shadow-child." Ginny's voice was carefully devoid of expression as she echoed Hesper.

"A shadow-boy, but I don't think it's really a boy or even a child at all. It's something truly evil, something rotten, that's taken on a form vaguely similar to Leon Oberman's— that's the artist—dead son."

"And here I was worried about your mental health," Ginny said grimly.

"I know it sounds crazy. I do. But look around. It's not just a spirit. It can affect this world, too. It's what broke all my dishes and trashed the kitchen. It smashed all my pots, and keeps me from completing any new works. It's the same creature that I told you about that locked me in the outhouse."

Ginny spoke flatly. "I saw your pills in the bathroom."

Hesper scowled. "Medication isn't the answer to everything. Being sad doesn't make you crazy, Ginny."

"I take it Richard is still around?" Ginny's voice was unexpectedly gentle.

"Of course he is. I told you he'd never leave me."

"Like this Leon Oberman's son would never leave him?"

"It's not the same at all. There's nothing dark or evil or hateful about Richard. He would never hurt me."

Ginny sighed and ran her fingers through her hair. "Yes, he would, Hesper. He wasn't an angel or a saint. He was just a person, and people hurt each other all the time. Sometimes by accident and sometimes on purpose. And you both hurt each other."

"You know I don't want to talk about that. We're past all that."

"If you were past all that, you'd be taking your pills. Your dishes wouldn't be a pile of dust on your kitchen floor, and I wouldn't be here. And neither would Richard."

"Why would you say that?" Hesper straightened, her heart pounding erratically. She clenched her fists, fighting against the surge of rage heating her veins.

"Richard did hurt you, but he'd have never deliberately tormented you. I would love to believe my brother is still here too, but I know he's not."

"He's not tormenting me. He loves me."

Ginny gestured at the house. "He'd have never let you live like this. If he were really here, and he knew staying kept you from taking your meds and moving on with your life, he'd leave. You have to know that. I know you do. Richard wasn't perfect, and he screwed up, but you're right about one thing—he really, really loved you. Seeing you like this—well, it would have killed him."

"If I hadn't killed him already."

Hesper sank down onto the floor, her numb fingers still clutching the broom and dustpan. Ginny leaned forward in the chair, clasping her hands, her face earnest.

"You didn't kill him, Hesper. It was an accident."

The terracotta walls, Ginny's blue eyes, the dust and glass heaped around her knees, all disappeared.

Sleet lashed at the windshield. The night was black and white, the road indistinguishable from the steep ditches on either side. Ice caked the wipers as they scraped back and forth. Hesper had to yell to be heard above the sound of the tires rolling through the snow and ice and slushy water.

"How long? How long have you been lying to me?"

"Hesper, it's already over. I swear. I broke things off with her last week. She just hasn't taken it well. But it's over. Over

205

because I wanted it to be over."

"How long?"

From the corner of her eye, Hesper saw Richard take off his glasses and drag a weary hand over his face.

"Three months, give or take."

"Three months?" Her voice rose. "You've been fucking another woman for three months, and I'm supposed to be grateful that you broke it off last week?"

Finally, Richard's hangdog demeanor broke, and his anger rose to meet hers. Back at his sister's house, there'd been nothing but remorse and repentance, tears and pleas. But she hadn't wanted him to be sorry. She wanted him to be angry. She wanted them to tear and bite at each other, to devour each other till nothing was left of this terrible truth. She didn't want him to be a sinner. She didn't want to be a forgiver. Even in the moment of betrayal and shock, her heart yearned to heal him, to heal them. To make this all go away. That was a weakness she couldn't afford to indulge. If he hurt her once, he'd do it again, wouldn't he?

If she gave herself a moment to breathe, if she gave him a moment to explain, she'd forgive him. She knew it. From the moment they'd met, she hadn't wanted to live without him. There was no tragedy their love couldn't survive. And that scared her more than anything.

She needed him to be an enemy, only an enemy.

He was talking, trying desperately to reach her with

words, his refuge always.

"I don't expect gratitude from you, Hesper. But I do expect you to be honest with yourself. Yes, we were sleeping together for three months. But you and I haven't had sex in six. So I'm not sure I really stole anything from you that you actually wanted. Maybe this is just sour grapes on your part."

"Oh, so if I don't keep you placated and petted like a good little wife, your vows don't mean anything? So sorry. I didn't realize you're such a victim of your manly longings."

"That's not what it was about. You left me a long time ago. And that still doesn't make it right. That's why I broke things off with her. She made me feel a little better for a while, a little less lonely, but you, Hesper, you are the one I love. You are the one I want to be with, even when you make me miserable. And I didn't like the person all those lies were turning me into. But don't pretend you didn't know, somehow. I sometimes wondered if you were even grateful."

"Grateful?" Hesper's voice rose to a shriek. "Grateful my husband made a complete fool of me? Grateful I slept every night beside a liar and a cheat? Oh, sure. Everything I ever wanted."

"Grateful your husband didn't pull you out of the world you loved better than him. Grateful he wasn't your burden or your responsibility for a while. Grateful you could go days without even having a conversation with him. Grateful he didn't ask you why you didn't want to have a child with him anymore. Grateful you could ignore him and know someone else whose name you didn't even need to know would take him off your hands for a while."

Hesper had never heard Richard's voice so bitter. Fear coated her tongue. She swallowed hard.

"You could have told me how you were feeling." Even to her ears, the words were pathetic.

Richard sighed. "I'm not going to defend myself. I did the wrong thing. But I didn't do it for no reason. And while I get this isn't the moment you want to admit that, you know we're in trouble. We were in trouble long before this. But I want to fix the trouble, Hesper."

The next words flew out of her mouth reflexively, without a modicum of truth behind them, only the desire to wound, to cut, to injure.

"Maybe you are the trouble."

A terrific sound, like the sky cracking open, made her jump, the steering wheel leaping in her hands. She'd hadn't been driving fast, mindful of the perilous conditions, but the sudden shift in direction was too much for the tires to navigate. She screamed as the car spun, vaguely conscious of Richard's hand gripping her arm.

Was it seconds or milliseconds? Her brain couldn't make any sense of the sensations that thundered over her. Later, her mind would stitch them together: crunching steel compacting into her body, breaking glass falling like snow over her face. Dry leaves and bark incongruously everywhere. Cold and wet gusting over her skin in gales.

She couldn't feel Richard's hand on her arm anymore. With enormous effort, she shifted her head enough for her vision to reach the passenger side of the car.

The crack had been a dead tree on the side of the road giving way to the weight of ice and the force of wind. A nightmare met her eyes: Richard's head nearly split from his body, lolling helplessly away from the fallen tree trunk into which she'd somehow spun the car perfectly as the tree thundered toward the earth.

Her husband, her friend, her beloved, her forever, lay inches away from her reaching fingers, but still she would never touch him again. The nightmare horror splintered in bloody pieces beside her was her everything and was nothing at all. Her own chest crushed by a pressure she couldn't identify, she couldn't even draw enough breath to howl.

"Richard," she whispered with enormous effort, but the wind snatched the sound away.

Darkness loomed at the edges of her consciousness, but she clung to the moment as long as she could. Awful as it was, it was the last moment she had with what was left of him.

"Richard."

He had to still be here, didn't he? Some part of him. There had to be a way she could urge his spirit back into his broken body, some way she could convince him to stay. Stay with her.

She rolled her eyes around, but no specter rose to meet her, no remnant of Richard stood beside her. How could he be gone? So completely, so suddenly.

"Richard…"

The darkness insisted on its mercies. The next time she opened her eyes, all was white and antiseptic and empty, empty, empty.

But Richard sat in the chair by her hospital bed, his eyes warm, his skin unbroken. His hand back on her arm, heavy and reassuring. Of course. Of course. He would never have left her. Never.

"We were arguing," Hesper said softly.

"You were always arguing."

The words landed like a slap. Hesper's eyes widened. Ginny didn't relent.

"It's true," her sister-in-law pushed on, no judgment staining her inflection. "You two fought like cats and dogs ever since I knew you. You were very different people. You loved each other, and I don't think that would have ever changed, no matter what happened. But you had a tough relationship. You have to admit that."

"I said terrible things."

"My brother did a terrible thing." Ginny spoke flatly, but Hesper knew the words cost her. "Men can be shitty, or so

I'm told. And it's okay to tell them so. You didn't cause that accident by being angry with Richard for cheating on you."

"I was the one driving."

"Because Richard had been drinking at my house. Do you honestly think things would have ended better that night if he'd been driving? The roads were awful. If anything, I should have insisted you both stay. But I was so ready to get the two of you and all your drama out of the house so Felka and I could have our own peace."

Hesper looked at Ginny as if seeing her for the first time since the accident.

"You blamed yourself?"

Ginny laughed, a short humorless bark. "Of course I blamed myself. I couldn't get you out of the house fast enough, even though I knew you shouldn't leave. The worst winter storm of the year, Richard too drunk to drive, and you too distraught. My baby brother died because I couldn't be bothered for one night, to help him and his wife through the heartbreak that was tearing them apart. Did you really think you had the corner on self-flagellation?"

"There was no way we would have stayed."

It was true. At least, Hesper thought it was. That part of the night was a blur of contrived rage and real, too real, hurt. She and Richard and Ginny and Felka were having their monthly game night. Very few rules and lots of drinks. They took turns at each other's houses and traded designated driving duties. It was mostly an excuse to overeat and horrify each other with *Cards Against Humanity* amid howls of laughter.

She supposed that, as much as anything, had contributed to the depth of the cut Richard's infidelity had made. He hadn't been wrong when he said they'd been in trouble for a while. Distance yawned between them with slavering teeth and a bottomless maw she refused to acknowledge for fear it would swallow them whole. But on game nights, without a word, they both suspended whatever ache divided them and fell back into the people they'd been when they first got married. They touched and teased, giggled and shouted, met each other's eyes as boldly and transparently as in their earliest days as lovers. Inseparable. Irresistible.

So, when Richard's phone had buzzed while he was in the bathroom, Hesper had picked it up without a second thought and glanced down at the screen, still mid-laugh at something preposterous Felka had said.

A mostly naked photo of a faceless woman. A message: *you know she can't give you what I can.*

Felka and Ginny had frozen in silence. They hadn't needed to see the phone screen themselves to know something awful had happened. Ginny had tried, fruitlessly, to take the phone from Hesper's hand, had tried to ask what was going on. Felka, the newest addition to the Dunn family, had retreated and started clearing dishes and wiping off counters as if that might make matters easier somehow.

Hesper had waved off Ginny with a grim fury that had quailed even the older woman. When Richard walked back into the room, a jovial smile still on his face, he'd taken one look at Hesper's wild red eyes and the phone clutched in her hand, and he'd known.

He hadn't even asked what she'd seen. Hadn't made a single excuse. Had spoken to her as if Ginny and Felka didn't exist, as if the two of them were the only people left alive in the world.

"I'm so sorry."

Hesper could still hear, could still *feel*, the emotion throbbing in those three words. How she'd wanted to believe that emotion was enough. But she refused to be one of those pitiful, gullible women who swallowed apologies like Valium and pretended their plastic lives made them happy. She'd rather burn the world down than be so predictable.

"Sorry?" The word was a snake, striking hard and fast.

And the battle had been on. It wasn't until she looked back, later, after all the anesthesia had worn off and all the lies everyone was telling her about where Richard was had sunk into her bones, that she realized the fight had mostly been Richard trying desperately to hold onto her while she tried to throw him off.

At any rate, Ginny and Felka would have had no chance

of convincing them to spend the night even if they'd tried. Hesper had needed to escape, to flee, to run away from what was happening. The cold wind and icy sidewalks had felt more like consolation than any soft words in that warm house. And Richard had been right on her heels.

Hesper walked across the room and took Ginny's hands in hers. "You couldn't have stopped us."

Ginny gripped her right back, her eyes shining with tears. "And you couldn't have stopped that tree from falling. Chance is stronger than us all."

CHAPTER EIGHTEEN

It was a kindness, Hesper thought, to let Ginny think her words carried weight. The fact that Hesper knew better wasn't a burden her sister-in-law needed to bear.

"Where are you staying?" Hesper asked, as if she didn't already know the answer.

Ginny snorted, unimpressed by Hesper's efforts. "Here, of course. I didn't travel across the country to check on you just to leave you by yourself in what can only be described as some sort of horror-movie set."

"I mean, I'm happy to see you, but I'm not exactly set up for guests. We don't even have an extra bed."

Ginny politely ignored Hesper's use of *we*.

"No shit, Sherlock. But you're not dealing with a fool. I brought my sleeping bag and a mattress pad. All I need is a corner. And I see plenty of those."

Hesper opened her mouth. Closed it.

"And obviously neither of us are cooking in that disaster of a kitchen. You need to get out of here, anyway. So, pull yourself together. I'm taking you out to dinner in Santa Fe. It's one of the best foodie destinations for states around. I'm hungry, and you don't look like you've eaten real food for God-knows how long."

"You just got here," Hesper attempted weakly.

Ginny shrugged. "I like road trips, sister. And the road

loves me. Get your shit together. We're going to town."

Hesper gave up. "Okay."

Ginny's voice followed her down the hallway. "That means a real shower!"

Maybe it had been longer than she realized since she cleaned herself up. She could have sworn she was washing her hair at regular intervals, but what was regular, anyway?

She weighed the shampoo bottle in her hand. She had to admit it was suspiciously full.

Ginny had brought something fragrant into the house with her, something fresh and cool Hesper couldn't quite name but breathed in with relief. Richard always told her she got lost when she got stuck in her own head. Had she taken a wrong turn somewhere, doubled back on herself? Did she just need a bit of thread to find her way out of the maze?

Maybe Ginny was the lady-in-waiting to her Lady, like in the tapestries, her hands full of flowers and sweets. Hesper snorted, coughing as she inhaled shampoo bubbles. As if. Ginny *might* possibly consent to playing the role of a snarling lion, but even that, Hesper suspected, was too secondary a position for her sister-in-law. Ginny and Felka were a saga in their own right.

At least it looked as if she had gotten the blood cleaned off the tiles, Hesper reflected as she toweled off, carefully avoiding the brightly illuminated gaze of the broken mirror. Assuming the blood had ever been there at all and not just a figment of her imagination. She wasn't sure what Ginny would have done if she'd found that mess on top of everything else.

She saw Ginny had scooped up her pills and replaced them in the bottle. That made it easier for Hesper to ignore them, at least. Hesper shrugged as she brushed her hair and scraped a bit of color on her cheeks and lips. She'd do her best to meet Ginny halfway, but some things couldn't be compromised on.

Richard sat on the closed toilet seat, his ankle over a knee, his arms crossed, his eyes steady behind his glasses. How well she knew that position.

"She's right, you know."

"Ginny's right about a lot of things," Hesper said lightly. "She's a smart gal."

"How long are you going to keep me here, love?" His voice was soft and low.

She spun to face him. "I'm not keeping you here. You're staying. You said you would never leave me."

"I said I never wanted to leave you. And I didn't. But I was taken anyway. As everyone is, eventually."

"Then how are you here now?"

Richard spread his hands. "Only you can answer that, Hesper."

She yanked the lid off the bottle of pills and dumped them down the sink drain, running the hot water as high as she could. The sink bubbled.

"How can it be real if I have to take medicine to make it so? Doesn't that fly in the face of reason? I see you. I hear you. I *feel* you." Hesper sunk to the floor between Richard's knees, clasped his legs in her hands. "The drugs are the lie. You are the truth. We're the truth."

Richard smiled sadly and stroked her hair. "You're killing yourself to keep me here. But I'm not here at all. Just like Andy isn't here."

"No. You're nothing like the shadow-boy."

"Aren't I?"

Richard held up his hands. Hesper gasped as cold terror swept her body. The tips of Richard's fingers were blackened. Sooty ribbons like ash stretched up his arms, curling and twisting around his flesh like some horrific vine.

"What's happening?" she whispered, frantically clutching at his arms. "Is Ginny doing this? I'll get rid of her. I'll get rid of her right now."

"Ginny's not doing this. You are."

"No. No." Hesper shook her head. "We're going to be okay. She has to leave."

"Listen to me, Hesper. And listen to Ginny. You're confused. Things aren't what they seem. But you do know the way out of this. You're the strongest, bravest person I've ever known. And you can set us both free."

"Why do you keep saying that? I don't know what's going

CASSONDRA WINDWALKER

on. I don't know anything. Except that I won't let you go."

"Oh, you will. One way or another. But you need to pull yourself together. Ginny's waiting."

Hesper's gaze skittered over the shadows creeping in rolling waves over her husband's hands. "Promise you'll be here when I get home."

"Me? Oh, I can't go anywhere, Hesper. You've made sure of that. I'll be wherever you leave me."

She tried not to hear the grief resonating in his voice.

Ginny was waiting on the other side of the bathroom door when Hesper patted the tears off her face and came out with a smile plastered on her mouth. Ginny just scowled. Clearly she'd been eavesdropping, but she didn't say anything directly about what she might have heard.

"I found a tapas place with high ratings, not far from the square. We can fill up our bellies and then go for a stroll."

The drive back into town was awkward, long stretches of painful silence punctuated by aborted efforts at conversation. But small plates and hot cheese and red wine loosed the grief-bound hearts and reminded the two women of their long friendship. Ginny told tales on Felka and Hesper found she had news of her own to share, about bright colored lizards and zipping roadrunners and the claybeds she'd discovered.

"So have you made any progress on deciphering the mysteries of the unicorn tapestries?" Ginny asked as she

219

popped a date into her mouth.

"I think you gave it all away when you explained the sequence hidden in the number of banners. I'm not sure why anyone questions it at all."

"Oh?"

"They're ordered one through five, and then the last tapestry, *A Mon Seul Desir*, has the same number of banners as *Touch*. How can that mean anything but that the Lady's one sole desire is what's found in that panel?"

Ginny smiled over her wine glass but said nothing.

"Plus, that's the only panel where the Lady looks remotely happy in. In every other panel, she's serving the senses of others. She supplies treats she never gets to taste herself. She weaves flowers for others to wear. She shows the mirror but daren't look in it herself. She plays music but isn't allowed to dance."

"I mean, those would have been pretty traditional roles for women at the time. Do you really think the artist who designed this tapestry was some kind of secret punk, creating elaborately beautiful images of a life he actually denounces as slavery while giving the Lady a way out in the end?"

"That's exactly what I think! Nobody, even somebody who knows nothing of medieval symbolism, can look at *Touch* and miss its blatant eroticism. And it's the only panel where the Lady appears in the position of power, literally leading the Unicorn out of the garden and off the field by his horn. That can't possibly be unintentional."

Ginny laughed. "You do know most people think that in the final panel, where she puts away her jeweled necklace, she's putting away all the physical pleasures of life and devoting herself to spiritual pursuits? Like disappearing into that pavilion is her disappearing into a nunnery."

"No way. The necklace represents all the trappings and responsibilities of her life as a Lady. Everything that was required of her in the panels where she serves everyone but herself. The world where she's defined as a daughter and a wife, and sure, a type of the Madonna. But she's rejecting that."

"I definitely like your version of events better."

"She tried to be everything that was expected of her, but in the end, she circles back to the one pleasure she found in life. She's not like the girl in those other unicorn tapestries that we still like to use today for wall decorations and pillows, a mindless little pawn of the war machines. She's not about to allow her unicorn to be slain or captured. I mean, it can't be meaningless that not a single reference to the life of men can be found in any of the tapestries. Not a sword or a warhorse or a battle or even a lackey to be seen."

"Maybe you're on to something. You should write a paper of your own, turn the art world on its head."

"Ha! I'm not a words person. Or an art critic. I'm only

good for squishing dirt."

"But you're so good at squishing."

"I am, aren't I?"

"So, are you going to follow the Lady's example?"

"What, chase my dreams at any cost?"

"Exactly."

"I think I'm doing that already, aren't I? I mean, I moved halfway across the country for the sake of my art."

Ginny refilled her glass from the wine bottle but only let the legs dance as she eyed Hesper across the table.

"I remember how you talked about this place when you and Richard first came back. You said it was full of old magic you knew nothing about."

"The Four Corners are a powerful convergence of earth and art and spirit."

"Tell me what you've been learning. The pueblos you've visited. The artists you've spoken with."

Hesper flushed. "I've just gotten here. I haven't had time to do much of anything but unpack."

"But you have plans? Contacts? You used to go on and on about how art was 95% listening and 5% work."

"Right now, I'm listening to the land I'm living on. I'll branch out eventually."

"Hmm. Seems you might need a translator. Are you sure you can hear what the earth is saying?"

"I don't think there's a cultural prerogative on the voice

of nature," Hesper snapped.

"No, of course not. But much of the appeal of this part of the country lies in the unique historical and cultural intercourses crisscrossing the land. The specific ways in which the people who settled it first interacted with it, what they learned. Lessons unique to this place and these people."

"Obviously." The word broke off like a split branch.

"I'm worried you're as buried here as you were in Evanston. Actually, you're more isolated than you were there. At least in the city, you were surrounded by all sorts of people and voices and experiences every time you hit the sidewalk or opened a window."

"I'm fine. I can't exactly show up with a briefcase and demand to appropriate a hodge-podge of cultural allusions to use in my pots."

"You know that's not what I'm talking about." Ginny grimaced but pushed on, undeterred. "And I have to say, the state of your house says you're anything but fine."

Hesper raised her hand. "Can we get the check?" she said as soon as the server came within earshot. He took one look at her face and whisked away.

Ginny fell silent—finally—but Hesper could still feel her gaze. At least being irritated with her sister-in-law meant she could let her pick up the check without an ounce of guilt.

In wordless agreement, they abandoned the idea of a walk around the square and simply drove back to the house.

It didn't take long to leave the twinkling city behind and be swallowed in the silent blackness of the desert night. Hesper cracked her window. The wind and the roar of wheels on asphalt soothed the blood boiling in her veins. Ginny cranked up a mariachi radio station.

Stars hung heavy and bright over the little hacienda and its ring of trees when Ginny pulled in and shut off the rental car. Ginny walked around to the trunk and pulled out her bedroll and a small suitcase. Hesper supposed that was part of what it meant to be family: you might be madder than a hornet at each other, but you belonged together, all the same.

She helped Ginny make up her bed in a corner of the living room and even offered up an extra pillow. She showed her sister-in-law where all the bathroom supplies were and set out a clean towel so Ginny could wash off her traveling day before getting some sleep.

It felt odd, disquieting, to have someone else in the house, someone still trapped on this side of the ether with her. Hesper wandered listlessly while the shower water ran, finding herself in front of the tapestries as she often did.

A Mon Seul Desir.

Hesper traced the threads with a careful finger. How could anyone imagine the Lady would resign herself to a life devoid of all physical pleasures after spending all that time serving the desires of others? Not that Hesper thought it was truly about the carnal versus the spiritual. Any work of art worth remembering breathed in layers upon layers of comprehension. That's where lay the power of art. Every person who came to it, came away with a slightly different facet of the same truths hidden in its representations.

So, sure, on the surface, the Lady was exploring the mortal life and its various incarnations. But more than that, she was learning the difference between a life lived solely to meet the expectations of others and a life chosen by her will alone. A life independent need not be a lonely life. The Lady would have the Unicorn as her companion, after all. Assuming Hesper was right. Which she liked to assume, most of the time.

So, what was the Unicorn? What did the Lady's choice mean? Sexual expression and fulfillment, surely. Hesper didn't care how many hundreds of years ago these tapestries had first been hung or how many priests had smiled on them, the erotic implication of the Unicorn and his magnificent horn were inescapable. But it was more than that, she was certain.

Society liked to pretend—almost now as much as then—that the physical desires of women found fulfillment at the command of men, but the artist who designed the *Touch* tapestry didn't truck with that. The Lady clearly wielded the power. Her hand grasped the horn firmly, her steps led the way, her gaze dictated their destination far beyond the bounds of the safe little garden to which they'd been consigned.

And yet the Unicorn was no humble and dejected servant. He stepped gladly and unhesitatingly beside his Lady. So, while the tapestry might be about sexual delight, it was also about power and will and courage, about abandoning all the safety found in the strictures of propriety and caste and stepping out to seize what was most dangerous and most desirable.

Hesper couldn't help but think of the old nursery rhyme:

The hart, he loves the high wood,

The hare, he loves the hill,

The knight, he loves his bright sword,

The lady, loves her will.

However much people might pretend to have imagined that women craved the so-called safety and protection of being treated as the weaker sex, Hesper didn't believe any thinking people had ever really believed that. Even nursery rhymes acknowledged that women wanted freedom more than anything else, and that the longing for it was as natural as the longing of the deer for the forest. And these tapestries, however discreetly, told the same story, as far as Hesper could see.

Maybe men whose petty powers were threatened by women liked to claim otherwise, but Hesper was sure they'd been as wrong a thousand years ago as they were today.

Anyone whose strength relied solely on the weakness or degradation of others possessed no real strength at all.

Ginny padded quietly down the hall to stand behind Hesper. She'd wisely pulled on a pair of warm socks. Who knew how many shards of glass still littered the floor? And New Mexico nights were cool, anyway, even in the summer.

"I see it," she said softly.

"I can't see anything else, anymore," Hesper said.

"Do you think she makes it out?"

"I hope so. She doesn't have the look of someone who turns back before they reach their goal."

"And unicorns weren't all sweet sparkles and tossing manes back then. They were creatures of war. I'm guessing if she encounters any danger she can't handle herself, that horn and those hooves will make short work of them."

"Yeah, I like to think so."

"Do you want me to help you put the doors back on the cabinets tomorrow?" Ginny waved a hand at the stack of blanket-draped doors against the wall.

"Oh, no, I'm selling those." Although even as she spoke the words, Hesper wasn't so sure. An idea was niggling in the back of her mind.

"Selling your cabinet doors?"

"Those are the paintings I told you about. Leon Oberman's paintings of his son Andy. There's a gallery in town that wants to help me sell them. Put on an exhibition and everything."

"Can you do that? What about his estate?"

Hesper shrugged. "Nobody came forward to claim the house when it went into foreclosure after he died. I don't actually know if he has much family. But even the bank didn't pay any attention to the paintings when they had possession. They sold me the house and all its furnishings, so they're mine now. At least, that's my story, and I'm sticking to it."

"Are they worth a lot?"

"I think so. The gallery owner has an appraiser coming out, I'm not sure when. Actually, I thought that's who you were when I heard the knocking on the door. Oberman's career was just reaching a pinnacle when he started struggling, and I would imagine these would have particular appeal given the tragedy of his life. At least, the gallery owner—her name's Matilde—seemed to be fighting hard to hide her excitement."

"Maybe you should consult a lawyer. I'd hate for you to be taken advantage of."

"You're probably right," Hesper agreed vaguely. All this talk about money was boring her. It wasn't Ginny's fault. Her sister-in-law was just worried about what she thought was her mentally ill relative, who'd always been a bit of a flake to begin with. If Ginny had seen the paintings for herself, she wouldn't be so fixated on the potential profit. Maybe Hesper should show her what lay hidden under wool.

Nonetheless, Hesper felt weirdly possessive. She told herself it was late, there was no reason to pull off the blankets and show Ginny what Leon Oberman's heart looked like splayed out in wood and paint and brushstrokes.

"I leave the fans on in front of the windows all night," she said, changing the subject. "It helps the house stay cool during the day, and the noise helps me sleep. But I can shut off the fans here in the living room and the kitchen if it bothers you."

"Oh, no, fans are perfect. I figure that's a sort of Turing test—anybody who can sleep without white noise is an android. "

Hesper laughed unexpectedly. "So is Felka human or robot?"

"Oh, robot, one hundred percent. But there are advantages to marrying a robot. They have skills, you know? And she humors my human need for a fan at night, so it's okay. We just buy extra blankets. All that circuitry gets cold easy."

Hesper chuckled perfunctorily at Ginny's attempt at casual humor. Washing out a glass in the kitchen sink, she filled it up with water so Ginny could keep it by her makeshift bed. "I'll be right down the hall if you need me. Don't hesitate to come in if you get scared."

"Scared?"

"I told you on the phone. This place is haunted. And not all the spirits are friendly."

"I should have brought Felka. She's got all that Catholic shit. Rosaries and crucifixes. She'd have your place cleaned out in no time."

"You don't believe in any of that."

Ginny shrugged. "I don't believe in ghosts either. I figure one would cancel the other out."

"I'm not sure that's how it works."

"Felka would agree with you, I don't doubt. At any rate, no ghost has any reason to be mad at me. I'll sleep like a baby. A chubby, middle-aged baby in a sleeping bag on the floor."

In the corner of the open window, long threads of shadow streamed from a dust-laden cobweb.

CHAPTER NINETEEN

Relief swelled in Hesper when she finally retreated to her bedroom and saw Richard waiting there for her, tucked up in the corner of the bed with Thomas Merton's *The Seven Storey Mountain*. He'd picked it up at the library the week before the accident. A better woman would have returned it, she supposed, certainly, before moving a thousand miles away, but how could she do that? He wasn't finished reading it.

She didn't even know what the book was about, what had prompted Richard's interest in the thick tome. She didn't want to think about whether or not he ever made it past the bookmark he'd placed the night before their dinner at Ginny and Felka's, if he read the same pages over and over again, if he would ever arrive at the end.

Maybe she didn't want him to reach the last page. Maybe it had a sad ending.

But when Richard raised his head to greet her, horror choked her with a cold fist around her throat. Where his mouth and chin should've been, black shadows moved over his skin. His eyes, as they met hers, were impossibly sad and despairing, but he couldn't say a word. Couldn't part the lips nearly lost behind the darkness.

She rushed to him, scrambling over the unmade bed to cup his cold face between her palms. Somehow it was more horrible to know the shadows held as much corporeal reality as his flesh. She ran her thumbs over the blackness upon his mouth , but felt only smoothness. Now, she saw his hands too, clutching the covers of his book, were completely shadow.

"No, no, no, Richard," she muttered, refusing to give in to the tears that pressed with hysterical frenzy against the back of her eyelids. "I won't let you go. I don't know what this is, that's trying to take you, but I won't let it."

Richard tilted her head back so he could look directly into her eyes. Something fierce and determined and unafraid willed her to understand, to hear the words he could no longer speak, but Hesper couldn't make sense of his intention. Couldn't, or wouldn't. She wasn't sure. She only knew she was being backed into a corner where there was no floor for her next step, but empty air and an abyss where her nightmares waited.

Gradually the grimness faded from Richard's expression, and he softened. She knew that look. He would give in. He would give Hesper her way. Whatever it cost. His chest shuddered as he pulled her close, as if he sighed heavily. Tightly he wrapped his arms around her. She nuzzled against his breastbone, but the peace his embrace usually brought eluded her.

She wasn't even disquieted to see Leon Oberman standing beside her bedroom door. Why wasn't he shadow? He looked as flesh-and-blood as she felt, though she wondered if that was real, either. Even the wound on his neck and the dried-brown stains on his shirt appeared inconsequential, nothing more than the aftermath of some minor accident.

"Why do you stay here?" she asked, pushing herself out of Richard's arms and crossing her legs as she faced the specter. "You know Andy isn't here."

Leon's face twisted, and the grief and remorse pouring from him swamped Hesper till she thought she might drown.

"I can't leave," he said. "I can't go to him."

"It's the paintings, isn't it? The paintings have you tied here, somehow."

Leon's lips twisted in something like a smile, but the effect was macabre.

"You're very stubborn, aren't you? Your husband is right. Or should I say you are right? You won't even admit the truth to yourself. As for me...I don't deserve to go."

"Because you made a mistake?"

"Because I chose myself over my son. Because that mistake I made cost him his life."

"Maybe you're not as important as you think you are. That mistake was one of hundreds, maybe thousands of variables that day. You didn't control the rain. Or Andy's immune system. Or the kid who maybe sneezed on him at school two days before. Or the red lights you hit on your way to the bus stop. Or the gust of wind that flipped out his umbrella. And the one mistake you did make, of forgetting the time, you'd give anything in the world to undo. Doesn't that count for something?"

"Does it?" Leon searched her eyes.

Hesper could feel Richard behind her, listening intently.

"Our stories aren't the same at all," she protested. "You were a father whose whole world was his son, who made one mistake that may or may not have contributed to his death. I was a wounded and furious wife who wanted nothing more than to hurt my husband at the exact moment that he was— was hurt."

Leon chuckled, a hideous sound. "Parenthood and its saints are a myth no-one should believe. Yes, I loved Andy more than anything else in the world, and I'd do anything, even now, to change our story. But he wasn't my whole world. No child is their parent's whole world. Parents, even the martyr variety, have a thousand selfish impulses a day. We want to sleep in, we want to eat that last bowl of ice cream ourselves, we want to watch something, anything, besides the same cartoon over and over again, we want to be able to go out and forget our phones and not worry for just a damn hour."

"Don't you hear yourself? Everything you felt is what every parent feels. Wanting a moment of life for yourself isn't selfish, it's human. And how many times did you still choose Andy over yourself, no matter what you wanted?"

"One time too few."

"You've got to know that's not what you were doing. If the choice you'd made had been between a few more minutes on your date or having Andy with you still today, you'd have chosen Andy without a second thought."

"Yes." The word was a low rumble of agony.

"Then, however much you might want to blame yourself, you can't. That wasn't the choice you were given. Fate never, ever, shows what's behind the second door. You already know this wasn't your fault."

Somehow it was Richard's voice that spoke from Leon's mouth. "You better than anyone should know the difference between self-loathing and the truth."

Hesper spun around, leaping off the bed. Richard was gone, and the shadow-boy crouched where he had been, malevolence roiling in the air around it. "Leon?" she quavered. "Richard?"

She glanced over her shoulder just in time to see Leon dissipating into nothingness. "Sometimes what we choose to hate is stronger than all the love in the world," she heard him say.

The bedroom light switched off. The only illumination in the room came from the burning holes in the face of the shadow-boy as it stalked slowly toward her.

"I'm not afraid of you," she said grimly, her hands balled

235

into fists at her side. "You're nothing more than the lies Leon told himself."

Laughter, beastly in its childlike modulation, ricocheted around the room. Hesper backed up, reaching behind herself, searching for the door handle.

"Leave Richard alone," she hissed. "He's nothing like you. I won't let you take him from me."

Her fingers found smooth bronze, and she twisted frantically and stumbled out into the moonlit hallway, her eyes half-blind as she adjusted. She slammed the door shut behind her, but the shadow-child skipped along at her side, undeterred. From one dark hand to another, it tossed Richard's book like a juggling ball.

"Give that back." She snatched at the book futilely.

The shadow-boy darted ahead of her, leaping onto the kitchen table and holding the book out of Hesper's reach. Unmindful of Ginny's snoring from the living room, Hesper jumped after it without hesitating. It leapt again, landing on the counter with a clatter.

"No!" Hesper howled. The sound of shredding paper filled the air as the shadow-boy ripped page after page from the spine of the book.

She was momentarily stunned into immobility when the lights flipped on, and Ginny's shocked voice sounded behind her.

"Hesper! What are you doing? What's happening?"

Hesper had barely managed to seize what remained of *The Seven Storey Mountain* before the shadow-boy disappeared through the window over the kitchen sink. She turned to face her sister-in-law; the ragged spine of the book clutched in her hand.

"I'm so sorry," she struggled to explain. "The shadow-boy...he was tearing Richard's book apart..." Her words trailed off as she stared in horror at the broken covers.

"Oh, no. Oh, no, no, no. Mastodon-munchers."

Ginny's hands closed gently over hers, pulling her fingers free and taking the book from her. Hesper looked around, stricken, at the torn pages littering the kitchen floor.

"Richard was right in the middle of reading this. Now what will he do?"

Ginny ignored the tears on her own face and spoke as steadily as she could. "Richard isn't going to finish that book. Come on, Hesper, let me help you back to bed."

"I haven't been to bed yet."

"Yes, you have. I came to check on you. You were sound asleep. Snoring, even. You've been having a nightmare. Sleepwalking."

Hesper shook her head. "No, no. I was talking to Richard, and then to Leon, but then the shadow-boy came and chased them away. Things aren't what they seem, Ginny. I swear. This is real."

Ginny gestured to the remnants of the book. "I see what's real. You can, too. Come on. I'll lie down with you. It'll be okay."

Hesper allowed herself to be herded back to her room. She couldn't blame Ginny for being skeptical. A shadow-boy with no mouth and flaming eye sockets wasn't exactly an everyday occurrence. Once Ginny saw it for herself, she'd understand. Till then, maybe Hesper should play along. She didn't want Ginny to decide she needed to commit her for her own protection. That could be a corner she couldn't get herself out of.

Although it might already be too late for that. Hesper knew she hadn't made the best impression. And once she made her mind up, her sister-in-law was a force to be reckoned with.

Hesper couldn't save Richard from the shadows if she was locked up in some mental ward in Santa Fe or wherever the crazies went around here. She needed to pull herself together and put on a good face. Chin up. Bootstraps. Something of that platitudinal variety. It would've been nice if she could have persuaded Ginny of what was really happening here, solicited her help in freeing Leon from the house and chasing the shadows away from Richard, but it wasn't necessary. Hesper could handle this herself.

But she needed to handle Ginny first. It was time to focus.

"You're right," she said as Ginny pulled the covers over them both. She'd turned off the overhead light but left a small lamp burning. Ginny probably thought Hesper was afraid of the dark. How could she know the ghosts here had no fear of the light?

"My thoughts are clearing up now. I think I might have still been asleep when you turned on the lights in the kitchen. I can't even quite remember what I was dreaming." Was she laying it on too thick? She hoped not.

"I know you're tired of hearing this, but you have got to think about taking your meds. You're overwrought. Tired. This grief is undoing you. There's no shame in needing a little help to get over the roughest patches."

Hesper thought of Richard's dear face being swallowed by darkness. As if she cared about shame. Or even remembered what it felt like.

Aloud she only said, "There's not. I've just been stubborn, I guess. You know I don't like accepting help."

"I do know that. There's a reason I didn't give you the chance to turn me down before I came out here. But I'm so glad you're letting me help, even just a little, now that I'm here."

Hesper hugged her sister-in-law. "I'm glad you're here. I've missed you."

She realized as she spoke that she meant it. She'd grown so accustomed to the voices in her own head, she'd forgotten how much she'd once leaned on Ginny's friendship. Sadness swept over her.

No sense being maudlin. She was glad, truly glad, she'd had this chance with Ginny before what came next. But that didn't change anything.

There was a way through. Maybe she'd have seen it earlier, if she hadn't been so stubborn. So selfish. But she saw it now.

Hesper rolled over, blinking back tears as she pulled the sheet over her shoulders. Ginny shifted and turned for a few minutes before her breathing grew deep and regular.

Tomorrow. Tomorrow Hesper would begin her goodbye.

CHAPTER TWENTY

Hesper supposed she should know better than anyone how easy it was to convince someone of something they already wanted badly to believe. And she wasn't alone in her subterfuge—her little entourage of spirits had their own reasons for assisting her in putting on her play. Ginny was an interruption none of them wanted. Even Hesper, much as she loved her sister-in-law, needed to get rid of her if she was to get back to her life alone with Richard and save him from whatever this darkness was that wanted to swallow him up.

So, they worked together, a strange cabal bound by shared interests. Leon Oberman kept to the corners. Now and then Hesper caught a glimpse of him gleaming in her own eyes in the bathroom mirror or walking by in the reflection of the windows. Richard had retreated to nothing more than an unseen clasp of her hand or the weight of his arm on her hip as she lay listening to Ginny breathe at night. He was never far from her, though. She could sense him in the rooms as she and Ginny cleaned or walking beside them over the rolling desert. She wondered, sometimes, why he didn't make himself visible to his sister. They had been so close. She knew he must miss Ginny, must want to talk to her, to reassure her that Hesper wasn't mad at all. But he remained silent and unperceived. That silence almost troubled her, but she chose instead to hug it to herself in secret, a proof of the intimacy into which no-one else could intrude.

Even the shadow-child had fallen into an uneasy armistice. Nothing broke—not that there was much left to destroy. Still, Hesper heard no lilting snatches of song, no eerie laughter on the wind. No slamming doors. He even allowed her to throw some pots. And that was pivotal.

Ginny wanted to be convinced that Hesper wasn't slipping completely off the cliff of sanity on which she'd only ever been precariously perched, but she was still no fool. Smiling and nodding and sweeping the floors wasn't going to be enough. Hesper took her pills in Ginny's presence every morning, however much she dreaded the bitter flavor under her tongue till she could dig them out and flush them down the toilet. Ginny sat at Richard's desk and read from her e-reader while Hesper hummed and labored over her wheel. She was striving for graceful, patient, peaceful, but she felt as garish and gauche as an operatic clown. Every contrived motion, every painted smile, exhausted her.

If Ginny was disturbed by the fruits of Hesper's imagination, she didn't say a word. Hesper had toyed briefly with the idea of recreating her World Tree series—God knew she needed to make that deadline. Didn't she? It had seemed vital, when she arrived here so recently, to pull those images only she could see from the clay. To offer something lasting to the years that would follow. Now that urgency had faded, leaving the distant memory of a duty, an obligation, whose import had withered.

On the other hand, she placed no faith in the shadow-boy's brief hiatus. The moment Ginny left, she was sure it would return with a vengeance, and she didn't intend to give it anything precious to destroy. While she might struggle to remember why the World Tree series had held such significance for her, she knew that it had. Diamonds might seem cold and hard to her eyes, but she wouldn't cast them into the gutters for all that.

Not that she didn't have a plan to deal with the shadow-boy. She did. Leon might not thank her for it at first, but he'd be grateful once the hated tethers that bound him to this place of grief and emptiness loosed their ties.

So, her work with the clay had taken on a new and distinctive voice, one she all but dared the shadow-boy to try and drown out. Fat, squat crones with lumpy breasts and glaring eyes, their gnarled fingers and ragged skirts full of bones. Life-givers, she tried to explain to Ginny. They take the stuff of death and breathe new animus. What looked ugly to the shallow gaze was only the high cost of creation. Volcano goddesses, earthquake maidens, the grandmothers who walked in the wake of the wildfires and sowed wildflowers. Greenskeepers of the universe.

Hesper had never fashioned anything quite so strange or so wonderful, and she found herself fascinated by the process in spite of its disingenuity. Or maybe she wasn't being as dishonest with Ginny as she thought she was. Maybe these weren't placeholders at all, and she was becoming something new. Maybe she'd found a way to create something that needed no defense from the shadow-boy, something bold and brave enough to stand up to the darkness.

Now was not the time for self-discovery. Though he stayed out of sight, Richard remained vulnerable to the creeping darkness she knew must yet be crawling on his skin. It took every ounce of will and discipline Hesper possessed to sit in the courtyard with Ginny and listen to her rattle on about Felka and furniture and philosophy and whatever else passed for small talk in her sister-in-law's rambling mind while her husband faded into night, hour by hour. Panic surged along Hesper's veins in a steady course, but she fought to keep her face bland and her voice pleasant.

Maybe it was wildly unrealistic for Ginny to believe that a quick visit and a few days back on her meds could restore Hesper to an existence the rest of society would consider tolerable, but people often do believe wildly unrealistic things about the power of love. All Hesper could do was feed that fantasy with every bit of acting ability she possessed. The hardest moments were when Ginny wanted to talk about her brother.

Ginny spoke of Richard like he was gone, so compellingly

and with such heartbreak that the old terror would well in Hesper all but uncontrollably. There'd been the briefest moment, months ago, when she'd first waken up in the hospital and watched those awful words—*Richard is dead, Richard is gone, I'm so sorry you've lost Richard*—form holes in the air as they left the mouths of everyone she knew. A moment when forever, black and void and endless, had yawned beneath her and snatched at her ankles. When she'd almost, *almost*, imagined a life without Richard.

But then she'd seen him, sitting in the chair in the corner of the hospital room, his fingers templed and his eyes smiling at her behind his glasses. *It's not their fault*, he seemed to say. *They can only understand so much. I'm not going anywhere.*

All the same, when Ginny talked about Richard being dead so matter-of-factly, Hesper's certainty occasionally quavered. Sometimes she looked around the room and saw herself, only herself, to navigate that hour and every hour that followed. When that happened, she would swallow down that emptiness like a poison and set her face in a careful mask of compassion and sorrow and hum quietly in the back of her mind, *you are my sunshine, my only sunshine*.

Anything to keep Ginny's cold and terrible words at bay.

And it seemed to be working.

Hesper even took her sister-in-law out to the clay mining spot she'd found and elicited her help in harvesting a new batch. It was such fun, and Ginny was so wonderfully incompetent and sweaty and sweary, that Hesper almost forgot she was only trying to convince Ginny to leave. She hosed the other woman down before letting her in the house to shower, laughing so hard she couldn't stand up at Ginny's shrieks and howls as the cold water struck her sun-warmed and mud-caked skin. Ginny reciprocated with more than perfunctory effort, which only added to the hilarity.

Swathed in bathrobes and fortified with glasses of burgundy wine and paper plates piled high with cheese and crackers, they sat together on the courtyard patio and watched the desert sun perform its nightly fireworks show as it bade them goodbye. A warm, aching exhaustion surprisingly like pleasure unfurled through Hesper's limbs. When had she last spent herself so completely?

"Are you going to let that Matilde person come get your paintings soon?" Ginny asked idly, swirling the dregs of wine in her glass and peering through them at the last ribbons of sunlight adrift on the horizon.

The appraiser had come by shortly after Ginny's arrival. Puffy and proud and overdressed, he'd been horrified to find the paintings piled in a stack of blankets in the living room. Doubtless it hadn't helped that the house still looked like some sort of failed refurbishing project. Hesper had found him painfully tiresome, but she'd tolerated him long enough to learn she did indeed have a fortune heaped there in the corner. Still, she'd happily bundled him back out of her home the moment his task was complete, without so much as an offer of a glass of water. She didn't owe civilities to pompous peacocks. He could buy himself some Perrier at a gas station, if he was thirsty.

"It seems the practical thing to do," she murmured noncommittally.

Ginny appeared to accept that as confirmation. "It will give you quite a lot of breathing room. No more worries about making the mortgage, and you can give yourself all the time you need for your pottery. Maybe you can travel through the pueblos, actually get to learn and listen and just absorb all the lore of this land for a while. See what emerges from the wheel then."

"Yeah. That's a good idea." Hesper popped a square of smoked jalapeno gouda in her mouth.

"I think—" Hesper noted how carefully casual Ginny's voice had suddenly become. "I think it's about time for me to go home."

"Oh?" *Don't sound excited*, Hesper cautioned herself.

"I see now you were always stronger than I thought you were. You have your medication and your art, and you already know people in Santa Fe. Maybe I was just anxious because your timetable for recovery, your process, was different from mine. I mean, I'll absolutely stay longer if you feel like you need me, but I think you're good. What do you

247

think?"

Not too eager, Hesper, keep it cool. "I'll miss you, of course, but not as much as I'm sure Felka does."

Ginny leaned forward, refilling her wine glass. "Seriously, though, I won't leave you if you need me. And Felka wouldn't want me to. She loves you, too. We're family, and we'll take whatever time we need to get through this together."

"I don't know if there really is a through. Maybe we just have to learn how to navigate a new landscape. But I am learning. And as much as you've helped, and as good as it's been to have you here, maybe you're right. It's time for me to try this on my own. Again." She chuckled self-deprecatingly. "Life has always needed me to make a few running starts."

"There's no right way to grieve. It's okay to fall down a few times."

"Thanks, Ginny. Really." Hesper didn't want the words to sound like goodbye, but she didn't want to leave them unsaid, either. "Thank you for being my sister from the day we met, for being my friend. For coming out here like a crazy savior to pull me back together. I don't deserve you."

"Okay, stop that. This wine is going to make us sloppy. I refuse to start crying on my last night here."

"Your last night?"

Ginny looked sheepish. "My flight leaves tomorrow

afternoon. I didn't want to say anything in case...in case it wasn't the best idea and I changed my mind."

"You mean in case I tipped over into the deep end again. No worries, Ginny. I've got my toes firmly gripping the edge of the pool. You can go, guilt-free."

Ginny grinned. "That's good. Felka has a whole thing planned for when I get in."

Hesper covered her ears. "Don't tell me! I need some illusions to cling to."

Ginny laughed easily. Hesper was relieved to see she'd apparently mollified whatever lingering concerns her sister-in-law may have had. Excitement burned under her skin, and she was grateful for the heavy weight of the wine in her belly. If she were sober, she didn't think she'd have been able to stay in her seat.

The image of the Lady, her hand firmly grasping the Unicorn's horn as she stepped out of the garden and across the unseen borders of her own true desire, rose in Hesper's mind.

I'm coming, Richard.

CHAPTER TWENTY-ONE

The following morning was the longest of Hesper's life.

Ginny moved slower than Hesper thought was possible for a human woman. Sloths looked like coke fiends in comparison. It took two hours after her sister-in-law woke up before she even put on her day clothes. She drank multiple cups of coffee and padded dreamily back and forth from her rental car to the bedroom to the rental car again, as if she were absolutely required to only pack one article of clothing at a time. Hesper didn't dare meet her gaze directly, for fear the wild impatience flaring in her own eyes would give Ginny pause.

Instead, she pretended she had work of her own to do and focused all her energy on not looking like she was rushing Ginny out the door. By the time Ginny finally draped her purse over her shoulder and jangled her car keys in her hand, Hesper had almost given up hope. She half-suspected Ginny was on to her and was deliberately dragging her feet just to see if Hesper would crack.

So, she smiled as sweetly and regretfully as she could when she wrapped her sister-in-law in a tight hug. "Drive carefully. You never know when a coyote or a roadrunner will decide to drop an Acme anvil."

"I'll keep an eye out for suspicious-looking tunnels, too. I'm going to miss you, Hesper. Are you sure I should leave? I can stay as long as you need me." Hesper had to give Ginny credit. She sounded entirely sincere, even though Hesper knew for a fact Ginny was dying to get back to her wife and her own bed. And air-conditioning.

"Don't be silly," Hesper reassured her. "I'm not taking the blame for ruining Felka's hot night."

Ginny laughed weepily. "I don't know why this feels so hard all of a sudden. I'll see you again soon, won't I?"

"Of course you will. Don't worry. I love you, Ginny."

"I love you, too. Richard would never forgive me if I let anything happen to you, you know that."

"Nonsense. Richard sucked at holding grudges. That was always my job. He forgave everything. But you have nothing to fear. I'm only doing good things."

One more tight squeeze, a gust of Ginny's orange-blossom shampoo fragrance, and the whirlwind that was her sister-in-law blew out the front door. Hesper stood in the doorway and waved goodbye as the little sedan disappeared down the dusty road.

"Well."

She pivoted slowly, unsurprised to see the three figures standing there, watching her with somber eyes. Richard's familiar form, though, was swallowed up in blackness. She clapped her hand over her mouth, fighting to hold back a keen of anguish as she took in his spectral form, all but lost to the shadows now. His eyes remained beautifully warm blue, fixed fearlessly on hers.

Desperately she looked to Leon Oberman, as if he could help her, as if he could help Richard, but he only radiated the same sadness as always, with not a glimmer of hope. How wretchedly unfair, that this stranger stood whole before her while her beloved husband was vanishing.

A high, wicked giggle rolled from the dark form of the shadow-boy.

Let it laugh. For the moment. Hatred flared within her, hot and fiery. Hers would be the last laugh.

"Don't worry, Richard," she said, though he betrayed no hint of anxiety. "They're trying to keep you from coming to me, whoever they are. But they can't keep me from coming to you."

He shook his head even as a hint of flame leapt behind his eyes. She didn't know what he meant, but she didn't have time to figure it out. Once the shadow-boy realized what she was doing, the fight would be on.

She crossed to Leon Oberman, grasped his cold hands in hers. "It took me a while, but I figured it out. Somehow you cast your own spell without even realizing it. These paintings aren't keeping Andy alive. They never could."

"No." His graveled voice seeped into her very skin, leaving stains of sadness. "They're me. Only me."

"All your own anger and condemnation and self-loathing. But it's time for you to go home now. Andy is waiting for you."

She dropped his hands. The shadow-boy skipped to her side, a peril horrifyingly playful. Its dark fingers scrabbled at her arms as she picked up the paintings, one by one, and carried them outside. Fingernails she shouldn't have been able to feel left long red furrows in her skin. She ignored the pain and doggedly held to her task. No sooner had she carried one cabinet door out than the shadow-boy howled with rage and dragged it back inside.

"Fine. It doesn't really matter to me where we do this. You can't stop this."

She left the paintings strewn haphazardly on the living room floor and piled the moving blankets around them. When the shadow-boy saw her retrieve the lighter fluid and a box of matches from under the sink, it screeched with fury. No longer did it sound like a child. The voice of a demon, ancient and rotten with malignance, reverberated through the house like a haunted bell choir.

It leapt on her back, pulling her hair with all its might, but she pushed forward, laughing maniacally as the streams of lighter fluid danced over the blankets and wooden doors. "Go ahead!" she screamed. "Fight me!"

Its hands closed around her throat as she tossed flaming match after match on the heap. Fire roared to life, and the bony fingers robbing her breath evaporated. Crackling and popping filled her ears as she gasped for air, her throat protesting at the acrid smoke. She tumbled backward, her eyes frantically searching the room for Leon Oberman.

"You are my sunshine, my only sunshine..."

There he was. Standing still and tall. Untroubled by smoke or flame, his gaze fixed on a plane she couldn't see. Like the gaze of the Lady, looking past the garden and the walls of roses to a world she would make her own.

This time it wasn't some creepy child-wraith's voice Hesper heard. It was the low, off-key rumbling of a father's bedtime lullaby. As she watched, tendrils of darkness detached themselves from Leon's body and drifted away.

"Thank you," he said. A smile transformed him into a man she'd never gotten to know just before he vanished.

Even with all the windows in the house open, she was running out of air. The ready supply of oxygen was only feeding the fire that now consumed three-quarters of the living room. Thick smoke nearly obscured Richard from view; he still stood, motionless, his attention fixed on her.

"Come on!" She ran to him, seizing his arm and dragging him with her. She snatched the *Touch* panel from the one wall that remained unscorched.

Together they ran, not out the front door, but down the hall to the bathroom. Coughing, eyes streaming, Hesper propped the *Touch* panel above the broken mirror.

"We're getting out of this mastodon-munching garden," she muttered. She'd been planning and imagining and replaying this moment compulsively for days. She didn't need to brace herself. She didn't need to decide.

She turned to him, ignoring the pleading in his eyes. She grasped his face between her hands and pressed a fervent kiss to his forehead.

Richard was waiting for her. That was all she needed to know.

Summoning all her strength, she punched the shattered glass so that a jagged piece fell free into her ready hand. Without a moment's hesitation, she plunged the glass into her neck.

The last thing she saw in the distorted reflection of the mirror was fire, leaping, consuming, where Richard's eyes had been.

—

Smoke curled into the early evening sky. Ash and embers were all that remained of the hacienda and its little ring of trees. Every now and then the remnant of a branch would pop as heated sap burst through the scorched bark. A few tongues of fire still danced here and there, but the desert had a way of putting out flames.

Hesper wandered over the apocalyptic scene, terror and confusion warring within her. There, in the center of what had once been the house, sat a shadow-man cross-legged on the glowing coals. Hell leapt in his eye-sockets. She scrambled toward the familiar silhouette, the beloved shoulders, untroubled by the roiling heat shimmering off the debris.

"Richard? Richard!"

A low laugh wafted through the drifting smoke.

"Richard isn't here."

Her skin crawled at the words coming so clearly from the mouthless, noseless face.

"What have you done with him? Where is he?"

"Where he's always been. How could you see so clearly what Leon Oberman did to himself and not see what you were doing?"

"No." She shook her head fiercely. "Richard wasn't my own guilt. My own hatred. He loved me. He stayed because he loved me."

The shadow-man spread its hands wide. "Even now you argue. I'm right here, in front of you. Do you really think the man you loved would haunt you until you were incapable of living in the mortal world? Even if he'd lingered for a time, he'd have left the moment he realized you were clinging to him instead of to life, if he ever loved you at all."

Hesper's tongue was dry with ash and emptiness.

"He did love me. I loved him. Love him."

The dark shoulders lifted in a shrug. "Are you sure? If you loved him, you'd have been willing to carry his story with you, instead of making up a lie that was easier to bear than the truth. Instead of admitting that chance stole someone you loved, and mourning his absence, you created a scarecrow you could carry around with you in his place. A scarecrow made of regret and guilt and self-loathing.

"And here we are. Dorothy and her scarecrow. Happily ever after."

"No. No, no, no." Hesper sank down into the heaps of ash and burning coals.

"Oh, yes."

CHAPTER TWENTY-TWO

Gloria Padilla hammered a *For Sale* sign into the dusty ground, curling her lip at the scorch marks where the hacienda had been with its lovely little courtyard and its copse of trees. God only knew how long this property would be on the market this time. Now it didn't even have so much as two sticks leaning on each other as an inducement.

She supposed the well was probably still operational. Maybe.

She should skip advertising on the real estate sites and just post the place on some paranormal internet chat room. Maybe she could convince some ghost-hunters to set up shop here. Some hippie psychic. She'd only even taken the listing as a favor to her friend at the bank. No way would they make back their investment.

What she ought to do was call a priest and have him bless it. Though she wondered if any would be willing to perform rites out here. The police hadn't quite figured out what had happened. With the presence of an accelerant, odds of the fire being an accident were pretty slim. But Hesper Dunn had been a city girl. Maybe she'd been trying to start a small fire the easy way, and it had simply gotten away from her.

But if that were the case, why not call for help and get out of the house?

Nope. Gloria Padilla was no fool. She'd grown up in the

desert. She knew the spirits here, and how powerful they could be. She didn't figure anyone would ever know exactly what had gone down, but she had no doubt Hesper Dunn had met the same end as Leon Oberman, one way or another.

Artists. Unstable lot, every one of them.

She snapped a few photos, for what little good they would do her. She couldn't drive away fast enough. That place gave her the heebie-jeebies.

She didn't see Hesper Dunn's face pressed against the glass of the driver's side window before she pulled away, her wild eyes desperate and pleading. Didn't sense the dark ropes of shadow entangling Hesper's body. Didn't hear the low laugh of the shadow-man as it seized Hesper's limp hand in its own and pulled her into a macabre, endless dance across the singed sand.

Printed in the USA
CPSIA information can be obtained
at www.ICGtesting.com
LVHW051729040324
773531LV00051B/1510